MW01231781

DORMANT
ENHANCEMENT

JACK RICHARDS

iUniverse, Inc.
New York   Bloomington

Dormant Enhancement

This is a work of fiction. All of the characters, names, incidents, organizations, and dialogue in this novel are either the products of the author's imagination or are used fictitiously.

iUniverse books may be ordered through booksellers or by contacting:

iUniverse
1663 Liberty Drive
Bloomington, IN 47403
www.iuniverse.com
1-800-Authors (1-800-288-4677)

ISBN: 978-1-4502-4695-8 (sc)
ISBN: 978-1-4502-4694-1 (dj)
ISBN: 978-1-4502-4693-4 (ebook)

Library of Congress Control Number: 2010932920

Printed in the United States of America

iUniverse rev. date: 07/26/2010

For Linda

"In an age of accelerating over-population, of accelerating over-organization and ever more efficient means of mass communication, how can we preserve the integrity and reassert the value of the human individual?"

ALDOUS HUXLEY

Prologue

"Warning that there is no 'quick fix' for the escalating problem of youth gangs in Los Angeles, Mayor Tom Bradley's task force on gangs has recommended a broad-based program of law-enforcement, additional legislation and educational programs to combat violence ..."

L.A. TIMES – Jan. 18, 1985

"Where do 'problem kids' belong? And who deserves the label? As fed-up parents issue a cry to quarantine violent students in schools all their own, educators are also fielding demands not to banish troubled children to schools too dangerous for learning."

MIAMI HERALD – December 6, 1993

"With community centers closed, public parks unlighted and city agencies shuttered Saturdays, troubled teens have few outlets to turn to, said the chairman of the Special Committee on Youth Violent Crime Prevention. The committee was started in January, after Boston saw 75 slayings in 2005 – the highest in a decade – with 30 of those victims under the age of 21. Another 290 victims were wounded by bullets, with half of those people hit by gunfire falling into that same age group."

BOSTON HERALD – May 16, 2006

"One in four teenage girls in the United States has been infected with at least one sexually transmitted disease, according to a study released by the Centers for Disease Control and Prevention."

NBC News – March 12, 2008

1

"Last weekend's gang rape at Richmond High School was almost bound to happen. All it needed was a spark – the elements were already there … All it took for things to lurch out of control, investigators, students, and community leaders say, was opportunity – and that came when the girl left the school dance Saturday night and walked by a group of bad boys boozing hard in the unlit courtyard."

SAN FRANCISCO CHRONICLE, November 1, 2009

"The National Center for Educational Studies will hold its annual meeting in the Fairmont Hotel in San Francisco on June 14-17 to discuss the problems facing our nation's public schools."

SAN FRANCISCO CHRONICLE – April 12, 2010

Aaron Rowland, President of the National Education Council, concludes his opening remarks to the delegates.

"… In the not too distant past, this group enjoyed the luxury of a concentration on traditional learning. But, times have changed, and so have our challenges. Gone are the days when we could speak with pride of our students' literacy rates, their curiosity, and their enthusiasm for learning. Now, much of our focus must be spent on such things as drugs, violence, lack of respect for authority, foul language, student apathy, standardized tests, electronic gadgetry, hostile and litigious parents, an ever-growing bureaucratic maze, a cowardly administration that justifies its existence by keeping its faculty numb in senseless meetings – but why am I wasting your time with a litany of issues with which all of you are more than familiar? You've all been in the classroom, and many of you have served as administrators overwhelmed by the endless paperwork that has nothing to do with learning.

"I know I speak for all of you when I say I'm horribly disturbed to see uniformed police roaming our halls or when I watch our students pass through metal detectors as they enter their buildings. The right to learn and feel safe in an academic environment is being destroyed by a few bullies and criminals. And what do we do about it? Expel them? Isolate them? I see you laughing, but I know there is also a tear hidden behind that smile. We learned long ago that we could not deny even the worst of the disruptive students his 'rights' by dealing with him any differently than we do the other students. We isolate criminals in society, but not in our public schools. Why? Because their parents leap to their defense. School psychologists line up with them in the name of 'self-esteem' and 'social promotion.' The media exposes education's failure to set standards as they carefully trace the declining literacy rates without offering anything like a real examination of the problem or the necessary solutions.

"So, what do we do? What *can* we do? Cower in the corner, fearful of losing our jobs unless we can appease the critics who blame the teachers for the failure of the children and demand we be fired? Dummy-down our curriculum so that everyone can succeed? Turn a blind eye to those students who are disruptive because we know the difficult road we would have to travel in confronting them? Teach the test so that we can point to our students' success, even though we know it is a sham?

"For the past several decades, academic achievement in public schools has been declining significantly. Compared to students in most of the other civilized countries, ours continue to lose ground. An alarming number of American students are alienated, unmotivated, and disinterested in what we have to offer them in school.

"And the causes? There are many. Changing cultural values, a failure by parents to provide the proper motivational direction and discipline, a school system in chaos, increased interest in non-intellectual activities, and on and on.

"Compounding this problem is the subject of our students' safety. Safety in American schools has become a major concern to all. National attention is now focused on crime and violence in public schools and on the methods of protection for our youth.

"But, I'll not dwell on this sad story. Let me report that a ray of sunshine has broken through this dark cloud that hangs over us. Two years ago, an exciting experiment was begun under the direction and supervision of a team of educators and scientists. It has remained a carefully guarded secret—until now. Today you will be the first to hear the results of that experiment—one that we think may completely revolutionize education as we know it.

"So, let me introduce the team that created it and the name they have given it: *Dormant Enhancement*."

I

A PAIR OF WESTERN GREY kangaroos lazily feed on clumps of hummock grass under the spectacular cloud formations that frame the rising sun. In the distance a ranch house and its outbuildings provide the only trace of civilization in the vast expanse of Australian Outback.

Inside the ranch house, Sharon Bradbury, dressed in blue jeans, a soft, cotton shirt, and Ugg boots, sits at her kitchen table sipping coffee. Her thick, shiny hair is pulled back from her face and is tied at the nape of her neck. Devoid of makeup, her tanned face reveals the presence of stress, causing her to take on the appearance of her favorite flower, a Cooktown Orchid, whose luster shrivels in the harsh rays of the Australian afternoon sun.

A ring on the mahogany tabletop made by her coffee cup grabs her attention. She quickly returns the cup to its proper resting place in a saucer before she attempts to rub away the whitish stain. As she does so, her fingertips discover a scratch in the table's surface, and the vigorous rub slowly changes to a gentle caress as thoughts of a happier time fill her consciousness. Years earlier, during the unpacking of the crates full of their belongings in their new kitchen, George, her husband, unable to contain his excitement, had taken her hand and led her outside to the spot where the table had remained hidden under a bed sheet since its delivery that morning.

Built by a well-known artisan in 1812 for George's great-great-grandfather, the prized table had been passed down from generation to generation before it was retired to a location in the corner of an old shed, where it remained under a canvas tarp for better than twenty years. Upon its discovery during one of George's vigorous throwaway campaigns, it instantly occurred to him that it would make the perfect gift for his wife as they prepared to occupy their new home. He immediately sought and found an old school chum who had mastered the art of furniture renovation. In a short time he had it looking almost better than it did the day it was built.

A smile warms Sharon's face as she remembers her surprise, excitement, and then wave of love for her husband. She pictures their struggle to find a way to squeeze the table through the kitchen door's opening, leading to a severe case of the giggles. Their attempts to push, pull, twist, turn, or lift, produced more frustrated amusement than success. Finally, their goal achieved, the two raised their arms in triumph before they hugged and kissed. Their joyous display of affection quickly ripened into a full-blown passion, and the table served as the most convenient location for its ultimate expression.

As the two fumbled awkwardly to remove the other's clothing, Sharon unbuckled George's tool belt, and it flopped over on to the table's surface. George quickly attempted to push it off the table and on to the floor. During the belt's trip, the hammer's claw dug into the smooth surface creating a horrifying sound. The two cringed as they imagined the damage done.

The trace of a smile gradually disappears, and her finger again follows the path of the scratch on the table. This time a grim image appears in her mind's eye: George's lifeless body, covered by a sheet, resting on the bare table. Her head lowers and her eyes close.

The picture, however, remains.

In an attempt to change the image, she decides to change her location. She stands and walks to the sink filled with last night's dirty dishes. On the counter rests an open 2024 calendar with the 21st circled in red. She closes it and tosses it in the direction of the living room.

Seeking a diversion, she focuses on something outside. Her look instantly softens when she sees the two boys atop horses too large for them as they herd cattle into a corral next to a weathered, grey barn. "Buns," the family's yellow Labrador Retriever, eagerly searches for a way to participate, darting in and out of the corral, ready to chase the gooey tennis ball when one of the boys takes the time to toss it. A smile gradually widens as Sharon proudly watches them direct the last steer into the enclosure, hop off their horses, and push the gate closed.

She looks at her watch, empties her cup into the sink, turns, and walks toward the living room. Listening all the while to the hollering boys and the lowing cows outside, she scans the photo-covered walls. She focuses on a recent family portrait and moves closer to examine it carefully. She studies the two boys, each with an arm around his brother's shoulder, doing their best to contain an impish exuberance, then the two happy adults who flank them on both sides. Finally, she reaches out and ever so delicately touches the man in the photo.

Abruptly, angrily, she removes the photo along with the others next to it. She hurries to the open packing box in the middle of the room and searches for a secure resting place for them. The task more than overwhelms her, so she searches the room hoping to find a less painful duty. Finding no such option, she returns to the kitchen and goes to the window to watch the boys while she regains her composure. Then she moves through the door leading to the porch.

At the barn the two boys, Eric and Brock, are busy removing their saddles. The roll of the genetic dice for the Bradbury boys has resulted in an interesting mixture of traits from both their parents in appearance and temperament. Twelve year-old Eric, the spitting image of his father, has clearly inherited an almost identical set of behavioral characteristics from his mother. Independent, athletic, adventurous, stubborn, aggressive, boisterous are but a few descriptive terms that have been used to describe both Sharon and Eric. On the other hand, eight-year-old Brock appears to be a carbon copy of Sharon in looks, but like his father is reserved, single-minded, sensitive, and highly intelligent.

Eric is the first to see Sharon coming toward them. With a big grin on his face, he waves. "Mom! We got eight!"

Brock, anxious to be included, shouts, "Eight, Mom! Eight!"

"Terrific. You guys are great."

"It was fun. And Brock only fell off once."

"I did not! The saddle came off."

"Who put it on, drango brain?"

"You're the one who showed me how!"

Sharon to the rescue: "Of course, Eric, you've never fallen off. Right?"

"Not that I can remember," says Eric.

"Oh, yeah? What about ..." Brock's defense crumbles as he intercepts the smile that passes between Sharon and Eric. He quickly joins the playful banter. "At least I didn't fall out of bed."

"The slat broke!" Suddenly a smile lights up Eric's face. "Okay, wise guy, we're even." He grabs the brim of Brock's hat and pulls it down over his face.

Everyone laughs. Sharon moves to help them stow the gear, but the boys wave her off. She steps back, folds her arms, and watches, pleased.

"You two left so early I didn't even hear you. Are you hungry?"

Both boys respond in unison. "Starved!"

"I've got hotcakes and eggs. And you both still have some packing to do. Come in as soon as you can."

"But Charley's coming," says Brock.

"Not till later," responds Sharon.

Eric offers, "Want me to take care of it?"

"You don't have to. He'll look out for us." Before moving, Sharon turns and looks back at her "perfect" house. A deep sigh precedes the unfolding of her arms.

Eric is the first to give voice to his thoughts as the boys exchange worried looks. "I wish we didn't have to go."

Sharon offers an understanding smile. "Me, too."

With a tinge of anger in his voice, Brock questions Sharon. "Then why are we goin'?"

Sharon hesitates as she searches for an answer that will make sense to a young mind. As she does so, she gently strokes his cheek. "Without your father it's just too much. We could never do everything that has to be done."

"Eric and I can take care of things. And there's Charley. We can—"

"I know how you feel, sweetheart, but I don't think any of us really understand just how much your dad had to do to … make everything work."

Continuing on his stubborn course, Brock announces, "I do!"

"Even if you could do it all, you two still have school," explains Sharon.

Brock gives a dirt clod a kick as he mutters to himself, "Crap."

"Do we have to sell everything—even the horses?" asks Eric.

"I'm afraid so, honey."

"Buns is goin', ain't he?" asks Brock.

"*Isn't* he," corrects Sharon.

"Okay. He *is* goin'!"

"I think so. I'll have to make arrangements."

"If Buns isn't goin', I'm not goin'!"

"Oh, Brock, you know I'll do what I can. But maybe he'd be better off here. It's his home."

"It's my home, too, and I gotta go."

Eric puts his hand on Brock's shoulder and turns him away. He quietly warns, "Not now, Brock. Back off."

Huddling into herself, Sharon heads back toward the house with Buns trailing close behind. When she reaches the steps, she stops and regards the house one last time. After a long moment, she quickly mounts the steps and disappears.

Inside, she picks up the coffee pot and fills her cup. With his tail wagging, Buns watches her every move and is rewarded when she lifts a piece of meat from a plate on the counter. She holds it between her thumb and index finger just above his eager eyes before she gives permission with an "okay." In an instant the morsel disappears, gulped down intact, with the hope that more would follow. His tongue remains ready for that possibility.

Sharon smiles as she scratches his head. "Oh, Buns, do you ever even taste anything I give you? What are we going to do with you?"

Buns, now almost twelve years old, became a member of the family during their first year in Australia when a neighbor offered the Bradburys the pick of their litter of six when they were ten weeks old. Sharon fell in love with the most active of the lot as he climbed over and around his mates on his way to receive her affection. And then, as he waddled toward George, Sharon's observation, "He's got the cutest buns!" stuck, and "Buns" became his name even before they made their selection and climbed in their pickup to begin their happy homeward journey.

When Eric was almost a year old, he began his first clumsy steps accompanied by Buns, his constant companion. As time passed, his buddy provided protection and stability as he took Eric's forearm in his mouth to lead him about. Though several hoses fell victim to his need to chew, his soft touch with Eric was a source of amazement for all who witnessed it. After Brock was born, Buns happily transferred his protective instinct to him. As the years passed, the three became almost inseparable. Typical of the breed, Buns loved company, was insatiably curious, and loved to explore. With such a large territory to roam and an extremely active family to accompany, he remained relatively trim in spite of his hearty appetite. Recently, however, it pained Sharon to watch his pace slow as a result of a hip dysplasia that she feared might gradually lead to a crippling arthritis.

After the resultant grief related to her personal loss had subsided enough for her to give the necessary attention to both its immediate and long-term effect on the boys, her real problems began. Many sleepless nights were spent searching for answers to a dilemma she had never envisioned in her worst nightmare. Without her beloved companion by her side to provide his stable support, she began to experience a vulnerability she never thought possible.

A host of worries paraded before her in a never ceasing progression each night. How could she … *they* manage to work a 10,000-acre ranch, particularly now after a long string of problems had left them financially strapped and facing a possible foreclosure? The obvious answer was to downsize. Sell and make a modest profit so they could stay? But, would merely staying in Australia make a longing for what used to be even more painful for all of them, particularly without George? Should—*could* the boys be taken from their beloved home without severe consequences?

Would a return to a familiar location she knew as a child—in fact, one of the most beautiful places in the world—be enough to help in their adjustment? And, with the aid of her affluent parents, wouldn't the boys have all the advantages they might not have if they remained? After all, both Sharon and George had talked about and planned for a university education for both boys in the States.

But, it would mean a return to a kind of dependency on parents she loved, of course, yet with whom she never seemed to agree on really important matters. Surely things would be different now, and she'd be afforded respect and independence since she was older and a parent herself. And what about this nutty dormant enhancement thing? An apparent revolutionary system of education that was quite successful by all accounts she'd read. Still, it was different from what she and the boys had become accustomed. Both Eric and Brock loved their teachers and were doing very well academically. New teachers, new classmates, and a new system—certainly a disruption for them and a cause for concern for any relocating child. This new approach was something she knew almost nothing about. She had promised herself a dozen times to do a little more research on its function but never could find the time or the will, especially since her mother had assured her that, as citizens of another country, an exemption would be in the offing. Home schooling was always an option if things didn't go well. So, as was usually the case, she let it slip to the back of her mind with the promise that she'd look into it as soon as possible.

Then today, Brock's question about what would happen to Buns brought another issue to the surface. It was one of the relatively insignificant problems she hoped might somehow solve itself. She had inquired about the procedure she would have to follow to have Buns accompany them and was told it could be arranged, but not on the same flight. Just how it would happen and who would take care of it was just one more thing that had to be addressed, but just not at this moment. Perhaps Charley ...

The only thing about which she was certain was the fact that they had the tickets for a flight leaving a short three days from now. And a thousand things to take care of ...

The sound of footsteps on the porch propelled her into action. She turned on the griddle, stirred the hotcake mix, and was getting the eggs out of the refrigerator as Eric, in the lead, pushed open the door.

"Charley's here," says Eric.

"Is he coming inside?"

"Don't know. Said he had some things to take care of in the barn."

"Okay. Well, breakfast will be ready in a couple of minutes. Just enough time for you to wash up."

Charley, who quickly became their best and most loyal friend, was the first person to welcome them when they arrived at the railway station in Gunnedeh for their "look round." From the first moment she met him to the present, Sharon could detect almost no change in his appearance and behavior. She had always thought of him as "an old saddle," comfortable and well-used, but always there and ready when needed.

After they had tossed their bags into the bed of his pickup, they squeezed into the cab, and Sharon got her first history lesson on her new home. There was, of course, an obligatory trip through town to get a "look-see" at the Dorothea Mackellar Memorial, Breaker Morant Drive, and the Gunnedeh Performing Arts and Cultural Centre—and, most important perhaps, the site of Charley's favorite hangout—a coffee shop where he could always find some of his best mates to discuss world affairs. They then headed toward the ranch house, a trip that took about thirty minutes, enough time for Sharon to learn about "the soils of the Gunnedah Shire, probably the most fertile in all of Australia, good enough to support both winter and summer crops."

During the trip, Charley dazzled them both with his knowledge of the past and with his style of presentation. "You see, the vegetation throughout the shire has gradually changed due mainly to the landholders clearing of the dry sclerophyll forests. The nutrient deficient soils of Australia supported non-sclerophyllous plants over most of Australia before the arrival of humans. The Aborigines' use of fire through the years led to the widespread occurrence of savanna, or land with grass. This left either scattered trees or an open canopy of trees. These trees were gradually cleared both to remove the competition for water and to improve pasture production, which resulted in what you see all around you ..." His almost encyclopedic knowledge and his manner of speaking seemed incongruous to his actual position as hired hand. In fact, he was far more than that. Just like his father before him, he was their most trusted employee, with the responsibility of supervising all the many and varied enterprises of the Bradbury Ranch.

Sharon expected to find him in the barn busy inventorying and organizing, as he had been doing the last couple of weeks. Instead, unaware of her approach, he stood leaning against a post staring off into space through an open door. For several seconds she remained quiet, reluctant to interrupt his reverie. Finally, sensing her presence, he turned and offered a friendly smile.

"Didn't hear 'ya."

"Well, you know me. Quiet as a mouse."

"Oh, sure. Never know you're around," he says with an impish grin.

"Looked like you were somewhere else."

"Yeah, guess I was. Tryin' to figure out just what it's gonna' be like."

"What *is* it going to be like?"

"For me? Take a bit 'a gettin' used to. Sure will miss you'n the boys, but I'll probably stay on in some way or another. Depends on who takes over. For you ... I don't know."

"Tell me, mate, do you think we're doing' the right thing?"

"Been thinkin' about that. Guess I only know what I'd do."

"And that is?"

"Well, this has always been my home, so the thought of leavin' it … well, it just wouldn't work. For you? 'Spose I can't quite see you anywhere else. But then with George gone … I don't know."

"I must admit, it's given me lots of sleepless nights. What effect do you think it'll have on the boys?"

"You mean their leavin' here? Aw, they're young. They'll adjust. My boys are at the age right now when they'd probably love it. You're the one who's at risk here."

"You really think so? I'm a pretty crusty old dame."

Though Sharon's comment was intended to be light-hearted, Charley's tone is serious and slightly ominous. "You sure are. And that's what worries me. I've never known anyone who jumps in with both feet the way you do. No fuzzy notions 'bout what's right and wrong. And with the courage to back it up. This place … our lifestyle … seems right for you. I know you and George didn't like the way things were goin' where you were before, and that's why you went lookin' for somethin' else. Now, to go back to where you were …"

"Funny how much we agree on this, but I do know that what we had here just can't be the same without George. And I'm just not sure I'm strong enough to be what the boys will need. It all seems just too big … too—listen, the thing I came out to talk to you about is Buns. Considering his condition, I didn't think it would be best for him to make the trip, but now I just don't have the heart to force the kids to lose something else they love. Could I ask a big favor of you?"

"Sure, I'll take care of it. I'll make the arrangements and get him to you as soon as I can."

Back in the house Sharon finds the boys in their room solemnly working on their packing chores. She watches for a few seconds before she heads for her bedroom. She picks up her cell phone and sits on the bed. She hits the return button, and her mother's voice breaks the silence.

"Hi, Honey."

"Hi, Mom. Got a couple things I need to discuss with you."

"Sure."

"Do you have a problem with my bringing our dog?"

"Of course not. We can find him a nice—"

"No, he stays with us. That's the deal. He's always been part of the family, and we just can't lose him on top of … on top of everything else."

"I understand. Of course."

"He's old, and I'm afraid he doesn't have a lot longer to live."

"I'm sorry. It's fine with us. Will he come with you on the plane?"

"No. Charley said he'd take care of it later."

"Okay. How are things going?"

"Still got a million things to take care of with the ranch, but other than that, we're plodding along. Mom?"

"Yes."

"There's something else I need to know. This dormant enhancement business worries me. I admit I don't know very much about it, but I think I read somewhere that there's a mandatory attendance for all kids. I know I asked you about this, and you said not to worry. Are you sure?

"Your father talked to an attorney about it. As I understand it, they wouldn't be required to—"

"The boys are at the top of their class here and happy as can be with their friends and their teachers. It scares me to think that I might be doing something that would jeopardize that."

"Honey, it's so hard to talk to you without seeing you. Your antiquated phone system is so—"

"Mother, you know how we feel about that. Stick to the subject. I need to know for sure."

"I told you. Your father has looked into this. He was assured that the boys were exempt as citizens of a foreign country. He spoke to Adam—remember Mr. Wilkerson?—and he said he'd take care of it personally. I'm sure you don't have anything to worry about."

II

IN MODERATE TRAFFIC, JUST OUTSIDE San Francisco on Highway 101, a sleek Astrobright, programmed to be completely self-directed, glides northbound toward the airport.

A soothing blue light pulsates in rhythmic harmony with the Bach fugue that fills the car's interior to buffer its two occupants from any annoying sights and sounds outside. Oblivious to both, Paul and Kristen Webber, an attractive couple in their late sixties, focus on their separate copy of *Newsview*, a thin, flexible screen fourteen inches by sixteen inches on which they receive their daily news. Today's date, Saturday, June 21, 2024, appears at the top of the screen. Paul scans the page and touches the corner of the screen to "turn" the page.

Now sixty-nine, Paul still retains his whiz kid mentality. He had finished head of his class in law school and, with the help of his father, immediately moved into a plush office with a prestigious law firm. But the perfect job was not enough to satisfy his insatiable desire to be the best at everything. His exceptional good looks and athletic ability even tempted him to briefly pursue a career in the movies. His penchant for acting, along with his success on the stage in several school plays, was enough of a stimulus to lead him to audition for the lead in a movie based on a best selling novel of the day. The callous rejection he received was more than enough to convince him that his dream of movie stardom was silly. He accepted the fact that making money was more than enough to make him happy. So, he returned to a focus on the law and established an enviable record of victories in court before he received an opportunity to create his own company with his best friend, an old college buddy from Cal. The two of them capitalized on the burgeoning computer industry in Northern California's Silicon Valley by forming a manufacturing firm of their own. Their combined talents, along with their contacts with several influential investors, served to make their gamble enormously successful. The two venture capitalists watched their fortunes grow spectacularly almost overnight. After his palatial home on the Carmel coast was finished, he and his wife eased into the lifestyle of the super-rich in one of the most beautiful places in the world.

Kristen was the perfect mate for Paul, and at sixty-five, her beauty still turned heads. From the moment he first saw her at a sorority dance on the Berkeley campus to the present, she continued to be the embodiment of everything he had hoped for in his wildest dreams. Born in San Jose, the only daughter of a banker and a teacher, she grew up striving both to be accepted by and to compete with her three older brothers. She chafed against the restraints imposed on her by her conservative parents. Due to the gender difference, her brothers were granted complete freedom, and this alone served as a basis for her rebellious nature. For many, her appeal stemmed from her confident and daring manner. She was easily the most popular girl in her class and a fun companion because she was game for almost anything.

Somehow, and perhaps in spite of this, she managed to maintain an outstanding academic record, good enough to earn an admittance to the University of California at Berkeley. The Kappa Alpha Theta sorority pursued her as their number one pledge, and she eagerly threw herself into the excitement of life on a university campus. It was two years later when Paul, taking part in the week of revelry leading to the Big Game between Cal and Stanford, accompanied a friend to a dance at her sorority. It was a magic moment for both, and they were married six months later.

Enthusiastically enjoying the opportunities their economic status provided, they eagerly sought to experience all that life had to offer. Travel, parties, and friends kept them more than busy and satisfied until the desire to have a family became paramount in their thinking during the fifth year of their marriage. A series of attempts failed, but finally Kristen gave birth to a baby girl, and they immediately set about to provide for her the same advantages they had enjoyed.

It was obvious from a very early age that Sharon, their only child, was a very stubborn and completely independent being. Doing things her own way became a way of life for her. At first, believing it to be a reflection of a keen intellect, both Paul and Kristen reveled in its expression. In addition, they recognized it to be a path similar to the one they both had traveled. Paul's admonition, "she takes after you, sweetheart," was often enough to assuage Kristen's concern. As time passed for them and their situations changed, so did their values and their behavior. Each harbored the belief that a similar transformation would take place in Sharon, but much to their consternation, they watched her characteristic obstinacy become even more pronounced.

As time passed, Sharon's choice of friends, activities, dress, music, books, and even goals seemed almost perfectly designed to disturb or, at times, infuriate her parents. To be fair, all of her qualities were not disturbing. She was clearly bright and ambitious, physically talented and confident, sensitive and aware, and fun. On the one hand, her parents admired her ability and desire to consider every aspect of a problem but were often shocked by her conclusion. To a formal wedding at her parents' exclusive club in Carmel, her choice of khaki skirt and tie-dyed blouse, totally inappropriate for the affair, was adamantly adhered to by their strong-willed daughter. The invited guest list, prepared by Sharon to a birthday party at their Carmel home, purposely excluded the sons or daughters of her parents' close friends. Instead, a parade of unconventional types passed through their front door and into the pool area to listen to music that made Paul and Kristen nauseous. Her fascination with the surfing life and her companionship with what her parents called beach bums created a high degree of anxiety for them. The views she espoused, based on the philosophical positions of a host of radical writers, occasionally amused but more often than not confused and irritated Kristen and Paul. They were delighted by her academic achievements but were concerned that she refused to focus on specific goals and future objectives.

Then, the topper: the "bloke," as she called him, who entered her life and almost immediately won her heart. Imagine their reaction when they heard the news that their daughter was in love and fully intended to be married as soon as possible—and to an *Australian*, the son of a rancher from a far off continent about which they knew almost nothing. The thought of losing their child was almost more than they could bear, and they resolved to do anything within their power to change her mind. As one might expect, the greater her parents' efforts to dissuade her, the more convinced she became that what she planned to do was right for her.

Paul again touches a small spot in the upper right corner of his *Newsview*, and the page changes. He studies an article for several seconds before slowly lowering the sheet and staring straight ahead.

"Should we take them someplace tomorrow?"

Without looking up, Kristen replies, "Okay. Where?"

"What about the aquarium?

"We did that last time."

"And Eric loved it, didn't he? How old was he?"

"Well … Brock was just a baby. So, Eric was … five. They might like to go again. Brock wouldn't even remember it."

"What else would they like?" asks Paul.

"What about the beach?"

"Sure."

Kristen considers several choices before she speaks. "Maybe the Boardwalk. That might be fun."

"God, is it still there? I haven't been there in years. Think it's changed much?"

"What's to change?"

"The young people for one thing." Paul raises his page and continues to study the article he had started before.

Without shifting her eyes from the print, Kristen quietly concludes, "Maybe that's not such a good idea." She slowly lowers her copy, looks at Paul, then past him at the moving landscape. "I talked to Sharon the other day, and she wanted to know about Dormant Enhancement."

"What did you say?"

"I told her not to worry. You had—"

"I had what! Kristen, I told you there were problems."

"And you know she'd never come if you were unable—"

"If I was unable to do what? Change the rules? Defy the law?"

"If she would only give it a chance …"

"Remember who we're talking about, Kristen. Are you the one who's going to ask her to use her 'common sense,' give up her boys, and trust the State?"

With no answer forthcoming, Paul continues, "I know how much you— we—want our daughter and our grandkids here with us, but this is not the way to do it."

"Do what?"

"Deceive her. Get her here under false pretenses because it's what we want. You know how she'll respond when she learns the truth."

"Then do something!"

Paul takes a deep breath, accepts his failure to change Kristen's mind, and does what's necessary to change the mood. "I'll try again. Adam said it was hopeless, but maybe there's something."

III

ALONG WITH THE OTHER PASSENGERS, Sharon and the two boys pass through a tunnel leading to a waiting area. As they emerge, Sharon's eyes scan the waiting crowd, searching for a familiar face. "There they are."

Sharon and the boys smile, wave, and head toward the beaming grandparents. Before they can take more than a few steps, a voice stops them. "Mrs. Bradbury, may I speak to you for a moment, please?"

Sharon turns and sees a woman dressed in a red, white, and blue uniform approach with her hand extended. "Welcome home, Mrs. Bradbury. I hope you had a pleasant flight."

Confused, Sharon takes her hand and responds in a friendly manner. "Thank you. Yes, it was nice."

"Those certainly are two handsome young men you have there."

"Thanks. I'm proud of them. Please excuse me, we—"

"We won't keep you more than a few minutes. We just have a few questions. If you'll follow me, please."

"What's this about? May I ask who you are?"

"Immigration. It won't take long, I'm sure."

"My parents are waiting right over there. Can the boys go ahead?"

"I'm sorry. They will need to come along with you."

Sharon offers a look of frustration and a shrug of her shoulders in the direction of her parents before she and the boys fall in behind the woman as she marches toward a bank of offices.

When they arrive at the door marked *Immigration,* their guide ushers them into the small outer office and deposits them in front of a desk behind which sits an obsequious looking secretary who immediately announces, "Mr. Contreras is in his office. You may go right on in, Mrs. Bradbury."

Sharon and the two boys immediately head toward the door indicated but are halted by, "Ah ... Mr. Contreras wants to see only you, Mrs. Bradbury. The boys can wait out here."

"Oh, okay. Be back in a few minutes, guys."

The office appears small because it is crammed with plants of all sizes and shapes. They rest on every surface—shelves, cabinets, chairs, and desk. Intense grow lights overhead create an almost tropical atmosphere.

Sharon looks around, but there is no one in sight. Suddenly, a large head with thick glasses pops up from behind the desk, sporting a big smile. The rest of the body quickly rises.

"Mr. Contreras?"

"Yes. How do you do, Mrs. Bradbury?" He looks around for a place to set the watering can he is holding and finally selects a chair next to the wall as its resting place.

"Please be seated." Sharon looks around for an unoccupied chair. There is none to be found. "Oh! Forgive me." He hurries around to the front of his desk, removes a potted plant from the chair facing it, dusts it off with his hand, and invites her to sit. Sharon remains standing and non-responsive.

His manner quickly changes from friendly to officious. He ignores her refusal to sit, returns to the chair behind his desk, sits, and looks directly at her. "Do you have any fruits, vegetables, plants?"

"No."

"Animals?"

"No."

"I need to confirm your reason for entering the United States."

"My boys and I have come to live with my parents."

"Mr. and Mrs. Webber. Carmel, California?"

"That's right."

"Very good. I need to verify a few more facts."

Sharon nods, and he begins to rummage through a stack of papers on his desk. "You are an American citizen?"

Again, Sharon nods. "And your boys ... the oldest is ... Eric?"

"Yes."

"Born in Monterey ... February 2nd, 2012?"

"Yes. When he was five months old, we moved to Australia."

"And your other son ... Brock ... was born in Australia on ... June 5th, 2016?"

"Right again."

"Then you'll need to fill out these papers."

"What are they?"

"A simple formality. Since your son is not an American citizen, he'll need permission to enter the country with you."

"What!"

"Your husband is deceased, I see."

"He was killed in an accident. Eight weeks ago."

"And you were forced to sell your ranch. Correct?"

"Not really. It's being leased right now. We don't know exactly what will happen. But you seem to have all the facts, Mr. Contreras. May I ask why we're being detained? My parents are waiting."

"Sorry for the inconvenience, but we must be constantly on guard."

"Against?"

"Against those who would circumvent our laws. Will you be living in Carmel?"

"Yes. Well, we think so."

"Then it's essential that you contact the Education Council in Monterey no later than Tuesday of this week." He hands her a card.

"May I ask what this is all about?

"They'll explain."

Fifteen minutes later, Sharon and the boys leave the Immigration office and head toward the security gate where Kristen and Paul are waiting. As soon as they pass through the gate, they all hug and kiss. Close by there is considerable noise. A group of about forty people laugh and shout to one another. Several carry posters that read, *Conniff for President*. A bit beyond, but out of sight, is what sounds like a brass band. Sharon and the boys' attention are drawn to it.

Paul offers an explanation: "The Nationalist Convention's being held in The City this week. Did you know that? It's going to be crazy there. Looks like it's already started."

"Sorry we were so late."

"What was the problem?" asks Paul.

"I had to fill out some papers on Brock. And we were questioned by Immigration."

"About what?"

"Something to do with the boys' education."

"Oh!" A stifled gasp from Kristen clearly reveals her reaction to the news. Paul hurriedly attempts to change the subject by rubbing the boys' heads and asking, "How was the flight, boys?"

Sharon turns to face Kristen. "Mother, what do you know about this? The man in Immigration seemed so—"

Kristen, most uncomfortable because of their close proximity to others, shushes her daughter. Paul, still intent on changing the subject, puts his arms around the boys and announces, "The boys and I will pick up the bags. You two get the car and meet us in front. Let's go guys." He hurries the boys away.

"Mother!"

"Let's talk about this later."

"No, now! What's this business with the Education Council?" She waits for an answer, but there is no response. "Is there something I don't know? You did tell me the boys wouldn't be involved in this DE stuff, didn't you?"

"Yes, that's what I thought." Kristen turns in the direction of the noise and appears to listen for several seconds before, "Sweetheart, I'm not so sure now."

"What! You said dad had checked with someone."

"He did. An attorney friend of his has applied for an exemption," replies Kristen defensively.

"And!"

"We haven't heard yet."

"That's it? You mean you talked to one person. God, Mother!"

"Honey, you had to leave Australia anyway."

"No! We didn't! We talked about this right after the funeral. Australia is our home. We couldn't live at the ranch, but we have lots of friends there. We love it! And I certainly wouldn't have risked losing the boys."

"Honey, you wouldn't be losing the boys. Dormant Enhancement's a marvelous program. You haven't seen how it works. It's been a godsend to this country."

"This is crazy! This was never even up for discussion. I would never have brought the boys here if I'd known this. I thought you were sure."

"Let's not worry about it now. We'll go see someone."

Sharon turns away, filled with worry and anger.

As the Webber car travels through scenic portions of the 17-Mile Drive near Carmel, Sharon and Brock are busy looking at the scenery and the homes along the Pacific Coastline. Eric, focused on nothing in particular, merely stares out the window.

With the car on automatic drive, both Kristen and Paul take the opportunity to focus on their daughter and grandsons in the back seat.

IV

THROUGH A HUGE WALL OF glass, people watch a monstrously large shark lazily traverse his territory. An ominous voice keeps pace.

> "... among the most primitive of any living vertebrates. For 350 million years they have met the problems of changing conditions by changing themselves scarcely at all. They continue to inspire in humans a kind of atavistic horror, an unconscious memory, perhaps, of distant ages when the sea held creatures even more terrible than they –"

A short distance apart from the others, fifteen well-behaved young people, between sixteen and eighteen years old, quietly listen and watch.

Eric is most interested in the crowd around him. He looks around often. "Mom, where are all the kids?"

Sharon looks around before she answers. "They're all over the place."

"I mean kids my age."

"You mean girls your age?"

Smiling, Eric allows Sharon her little joke. "Well, maybe."

"I don't know. Probably in school."

"But it's Sunday."

"You know about Dormant Enhancement."

"Yeah, a little. But are they there every day?"

"Apparently."

"But ... for four years?"

Kristen, standing behind the two and listening all the while to their conversation, points to the group of young people, "Those are DE graduates over there. And don't they seem nice?"

Huddled together and independent from the rest, the former students display no outward sign of emotion as they devote their full attention to their tour guide. At the conclusion of the description, their guide moves away from the shark tank, and without a word, his flock follows his lead.

"Octopus, Mom! Hurry up." Brock scoots to the front of the large group as they move in the direction of the next attraction. Kristen and Paul hurry to keep up with him. Eric and Sharon remain where they are and continue to watch the shark. Sharon tenderly places her hand on Eric's shoulder.

"Miss your friends?"

In response, Eric shrugs his shoulders. Sharon continues, "Maybe Robbie could come for a visit. Wouldn't that be nice?"

Again, Eric shrugs his shoulders. Without another word, the two slowly move in the direction of the group.

On the huge Webber front lawn in front of a magnificent mansion shrouded in trees behind a stone entry, Eric, Brock, and Paul play three-cornered catch. A car slowly makes its way up the driveway and stops in front of the three. A very attractive young woman gets out, sees Paul, and walks toward him sporting a dental-ad smile.

"Pardon me, is this the Webber residence?"

Paul drops his mitt and meets her halfway. "Yes. I'm Paul Webber. May I help you?"

"How do you do, Mr. Webber? I'm Kathy Kerns. Is a Mrs. Bradbury staying with you?"

"Yes. She's my daughter."

"Is she here now?"

"She's inside with my wife. I'll—"

"Don't let me interfere with your game. I can find my way. Nice to have met you." Ms. Kerns walks to the front door and rings the bell. The three suspend their practice to watch as she waits. When she disappears into the house, Paul, frowning, returns to their play.

Sharon and Ms. Kerns sit facing one another in the spacious Webber living room, watching the three major leaguers through the enormous picture window with the Pacific Ocean in the background. Ms. Kerns is the first to speak. "That's a handsome group on the front lawn. I assume those are your two boys."

As though considering the consequences of her answer, Sharon does not respond immediately. Finally, in a carefully measured tone, "Yes."

"I apologize for invading your privacy, but it's essential that you begin the orientation for your son as soon as possible."

"Orientation?"

"Eric's almost five months past the age when he should have entered the program."

The tone of Sharon's voice now reveals a rising irritation. "We're Australian. I was led to believe that my boys were exempt from this DE thing."

"But Eric was born in the United States. The law's pretty clear on that point. You were notified by Immigration that you were required to appear no later than Tuesday of this week, weren't you? This is Thursday."

"We just arrived on Saturday. And we're expected to be somewhere on Tuesday? Wouldn't you say that's a bit soon?"

Ms. Kerns' soothing voice is in marked contrast to Sharon's strident pitch. "Perhaps, but this is in your best interest. We want to avoid any detrimental effects to Eric's development."

"He's developing just fine."

"That's another issue. I'm here to inform you of the law. There can be some rather serious consequences."

"Is this a threat?"

"Mrs. Bradbury—"

Sharon stands and moves toward the entry hall. She comes to an abrupt stop and turns to face the unwelcome visitor. "Never mind. Tell your people I'll be there tomorrow. I want to get this settled."

V

WITH THE CAR ON AUTOMATIC, Sharon takes a good look at the exterior of the large five-story structure set on about ten acres. The grounds surrounding it are scrupulously landscaped. Two gardeners busily trim a hedge, and two others plant flowers near the front of the building.

Sharon has no trouble finding a parking place near the front door. She gets out of the car and looks around. Over the two large front doors are inscribed the words, *Monterey Peninsula Academe Integral.*

Moments later, Sharon enters a large office in which many decorative touches indicate extravagance and self-indulgence. Two walls consist of floor-to-ceiling books, except for one magnificent painting of the Monterey coastline in the center.

In the middle of the room rests a huge mahogany desk. The remaining wall is almost all glass, providing a view of the ocean in the distance. Flanking one side of a wet bar is a fish tank. In it, dozens of gloriously colorful tropical fish pursue the food being dropped by a large, imposing figure hunched over them. Without looking up, the figure poses a question.

"Do you like tropical fish?"

"No." Sharon's tone is cold and detached.

The man looks over his shoulder, slowly straightens, and turns to face Sharon. "May I get you something? A cup of coffee?"

"No, thank you."

The hulk of a man, appearing almost comic in his expensive Heritage suit, moves to his desk and with a gesture invites Sharon to take a seat on the other side. She refuses his offer and remains standing.

"I'm Dr. Thornberg, Mrs. Bradbury. I was quite surprised we didn't see you on Tuesday."

"We just got here Saturday. We're still getting settled in. The boys wanted to spend some time with their grandparents, for God's sake."

"I can appreciate that. I'm sure you can also appreciate our concern for the well-being of your son ... Eric, isn't it?" Sharon nods. Dr. Thornberg continues. "He's already several months behind."

24

In a voice denoting a firm resolve, Sharon announces, "Dr. Thornberg, let me get right to the point. I don't want Eric in the program."

"Why?"

"I lost my husband eight weeks ago, so I can't stand the thought of losing my boy."

"Please, won't you have a seat?"

Sharon's defenses remain intact. "I prefer to stand."

"You'll not be losing your boy, Mrs. Bradbury. Just how much do you know about Dormant Enhancement?"

"I know it means I would be turning my boy over to someone like you."

"You left the country ... let's see, in 2012. Correct?" Sharon nods. Dr. Thornberg continues, "Then you still have a pretty clear memory of what things were like, I trust. I'm sure you even recall the early experiments with DE."

"A little, I think."

"At first it was for the incorrigibles—the drug addicts, members of gangs, kids with criminal records—the ones society couldn't deal with, and their numbers were growing alarmingly." He opens a folder on his desk and refers to some papers he removes from it. "It's not surprising you don't remember much of this. You were a good student ... well adjusted."

"Something like that."

"So why would you pay much attention to these kids? We managed to take society's rejects—kids who didn't have a chance—kids who ended up in prison or dead in some alley of a drug overdose, and we re-structured their lives and made them productive members of society."

Sharon remains impassive as Thornberg pounds home his argument. "Actually it was parents just like yours who eventually made the program possible for everyone."

"You lost me."

Thornberg rises, picks up a packet of food, and walks to the fish tank. "Stop and think. Seeing the enormous benefits being handed to the miscreants, how could the affluent parents not want the same advantages for their kids?"

"Advantages?"

"Of course. A superior education, an elimination of all negative influences, a safe environment."

Sharon answers sarcastically, "And DE did all that!"

"Well ... yes, as a matter of fact, it did. We tried to get the kids at an earlier age, but parents still enjoyed their young children too much. That is, until the generation of 'tweens' began to exhibit teen behavior at its most troubling."

"Tweens?"

"Kids between eight and twelve. They were becoming every bit as difficult as the teenagers. Still, the earliest age we could negotiate their entrance into the program was twelve."

"That's crazy!"

"Society didn't think so. The causes for this behavior were fairly obvious—parental absence, a sexualized and glitzy media-driven marketplace, a growing peer group influence, and lots more—but as is usually the case, the parents were quite content to turn their problems over to others."

"Certainly not true in our family."

Thornberg appears to ignore Sharon's comment, but he abandons his fish, returns to his desk, picks up a folder, and faces Sharon. "Enough talk, Mrs. Bradbury. Let me show you what it looks like. May I assume you've not seen Dormant Enhancement in operation?"

"I've read a little about it."

"You have to see it up close."

Sharon and Thornberg slowly walk down a corridor in the Academe as he continues to explain how everything works. "Please understand that the students are introduced to the program very gradually. Beginning at age nine, they're brought together twice a year for a few days to give them an idea of what to expect. It eases any anxieties they may have, and it even creates some excitement about what's to come."

"Excitement? About being removed from the world?"

Thornberg stops to look at Sharon and laugh. "I can see you have a lot to learn. Let's start here." They approach a door marked *Orientation*, and he invites her to enter. She does so reluctantly.

Situated around the outside perimeter of the circle are fifty upright and empty "cubicles" facing the center of the room. Each cell is about four feet wide by seven feet tall. Its front is convex, and the lower three feet is glass. The room is lighted by a single spot focused on a circular control panel located in the center of the room.

Thornberg walks to the panel and touches the board. Instantly, the room brightens with gradually changing rainbow colors coming from the domed ceiling.

He explains, "This is one of the rooms we use for the introduction I spoke about. It's also used for orientation. Please … be a twelve year old for a few minutes."

Thornberg presses a button, and the front of one of the cubicles slowly rises. As it does so, its inside lights up, revealing an upholstered interior. He invites Sharon to enter. She merely stares at the open front. "It won't hurt."

Sharon remains rigid for several seconds before entering. She turns and faces outward as she leans against the padded interior. The front slowly lowers, seals itself, and the cubicle tilts backward to a thirty-degree angle.

As Sharon studies the pod's interior, a virtual reality screen slowly rotates down to engulf the front portion of her head. The light within the cubicle gradually dims.

Thornberg continues to guide her through the experience. "Now, Mrs. Bradbury, keep in mind that the youngster who steps into that pod would have been well prepared for the experience."

Sharon is now surrounded by images on the screen—a montage of colorful and exciting scenes: youngsters traveling by various means (boat, plane, camel, bicycle, etc.) to exotic places, and glimpses of enjoyable activities (sporting events, concerts, laugh-filled conversations, games, etc.), all enhanced by music in surround sound.

After a few minutes, the picture fades, the pod returns to an upright position, and the front opens. Sharon steps out slowly, doing her best to maintain a poker face to cover her exhilaration.

"Please understand, Mrs. Bradbury, that this is only a taste. Now, let me show you some students at work."

Sharon and Dr. Thornberg enter a room, rectangular in shape and approximately seventy-five feet by fifty feet in size. In it there are sixty pods, each housing a student. A control panel rests in the middle, with thirty pods, alternately staggered and tilted back at thirty degrees, facing it on each side of the room. Each houses a student. Though Sharon is fascinated, she lingers near the door as Thornberg approaches the technician seated at the central control panel.

"Hello, Frank."

"Good morning, Dr. Thornberg."

"What's the program?"

Frank touches a button on the panel and a rapidly progressing series of algebraic equations appear on the screen above.

"Trigonometry, I see."

Sharon gasps. "My God! How do they follow that?"

"You see, our conscious mind is capable of handling only a portion of what we can process in the state of dormant enhancement. Not so long ago it took a student a semester to learn what these kids will learn in one week. And, these students will learn it a lot better."

Sharon appears doubtful. "But … are they cooped up like this all day?"

"Cooped up?" Thornberg smiles and looks at Frank. "They visit many different places every day. They stroll the halls of the Louvre, they climb the Pilatus, picnic at the foot of Mt. Kilimanjaro—yes, even explore the

Outback of Australia. Oh, it's visual and mental, of course, but they *are* there. Dormant Enhancement creates a complete range of experiences they could never actually have."

Sharon, refusing to be taken in, looks away.

Thornberg continues, "They have dates. They go to dances, picnics, parties … without drugs, without liquor. And, without someone's car getting wrapped around a tree."

"And you do all that right here? Impossible." Sharon looks around the room. "There isn't even enough room."

"Tell me, Mrs. Bradbury, can you see the living room in your ranch house back in Australia?"

Confused as to the relevance of the question, she is not immediately forthcoming with her answer. When she speaks, it is tinged with sarcasm. "I'm afraid it's just a little too far away."

"Really? If you were asked, could you describe it—*see it* in your mind?"

"Sure, but I'm certainly not there."

"Oh, but you are. A good part of our everyday life is spent visualizing. It can be just as real as anything you can actually touch."

Sharon's resolve suddenly surfaces, and she announces in a loud voice, "Dr. Thornberg, I'm sure your program is … fine, for others. But it's not for my boys. They've been raised to be independent, and their education has been exceptional. I will mold my boy's character. He will remain at home with me."

"I'm afraid you don't understand. His attendance is a matter of law. All children must enter the school on the Monday after their twelfth birthday."

"But that can't be true for everyone."

"I'm afraid it is. We've had compulsory education in this country as far back as 1918. At that time all states required children to receive an education."

"What about home schooling?"

"That disappeared in 2018. Attendance at a certified institution is now required by law, and defiance of that law carries with it severe penalties."

"But we're Australians."

"Not quite. Eric was five months old when you moved. He still retains his American citizenship. As such, he's subject to the laws of the United States."

Sharon's eyes flash. "As I remember, freedom is what the United States is all about!"

"Freedom? Freedom from what? All the advantages we offer? Education … safety … direction—"

"That's for me—and him—to decide."

"Your selfish attitude is—"

"Selfish! Eric's *my* child, not yours!"

VI

AS SHARON STEERS THE CAR manually, tears of anger and frustration obscure her vision, causing her to drive erratically. She wipes her face with her hand, her sleeve. The sound of a car horn shocks her back into an awareness of her surroundings. She regains control and pulls off the road on the ocean side near the edge of a cliff.

Her head remains resting on the steering wheel while she struggles to get hold of herself. Finally, she lifts her head and looks around. With no one in sight, she opens the door, eases out of her seat, and walks to the edge of the cliff. She stares out to sea as she tries to calm down.

Her attention is drawn to a volleyball game in progress on the beach below. Interested, she drops to her knees to be in a more comfortable position to watch. A dozen young people laugh and shout as they run, jump, dive, and slap the ball back and forth over the net. Towels, ice chests, and discarded beachwear surround the lines drawn in the sand to create a court.

Sharon's concentration on the fun below momentarily replaces her troubled thoughts, but it also stimulates a memory of another time and place. Another sand court appears in her mind's eye, now with a large crowd of spectators gathered at Cowell's Beach in Santa Cruz to watch the four sweaty, scantily clad women do battle. A banner, supported by two wooden posts, reads, *2007 Nor Cal Women's Open*.

During a timeout, Sharon and Lynn, her partner, with hands on their knees and their heads touching, struggle to reach down and find an untapped reserve of will.

"Jesus, Lynn, we can't let it get away from us now. One stop!"

Through gritted teeth, a scream explodes from Lynn, "Do it!"

Across the net, their opponents take their positions, ready to score the tying point. Stationed several yards back from the line, the server begins her approach. Two feet from the line she rises high into the air for an awesome jump serve.

A diving Sharon manages a one-hand dig inches above the surface of sand. The ball rebounds off her fist in the direction of her waiting partner. Lynn, ready, bends low underneath it, her fingertips positioned for the return. Sharon scrambles to her feet, takes two steps back to make room to achieve the necessary momentum for her leap as soon as Lynn makes what Sharon knows will be a perfect set. Sharon's precise timing, aided by a spurt of adrenalin, puts her high above the top of the net, and she spikes the ball to a spot on the seam between the two frustrated competitors.

Sharon and Lynn become airborne, their hands reaching for the sky. A quick hug and slapped hands precede a strange quiet that falls over the two. Each searches for the look of resolve in the other's eyes. Quietly, but firmly, Sharon gives voice to their need: "One more."

Lynn walks resolutely to her spot near the net as Sharon gets the ball and jogs to her takeoff area behind the end line. Sharon takes a long look at Lynn, who is holding a closed fist behind her as she faces the net. The strategy set, Sharon begins her approach. The vicious jump serve, perfectly directed, barely clips the left sideline, inches out of reach of the diving opponent.

A short while later, in the midst of several friends squatted around a monstrous cooler next to a handsome trophy, Sharon and Lynn gleefully replay their favorite shots. With Lynn on her feet demonstrating a favorite technique, Sharon notices two young men, dressed in cutoffs, t-shirts with the logo *Kangaroos–Rugby*, and Australian bush hats, approach the group. She is the first to speak.

"Hi, guys. What's happening?"

"G'day." The taller of the two flashes a wide smile and tips his hat. "Name's George, and this is my mate, Dennis. You ladies played a ripper of a game. Dennis, here, said you'd tell us to rack off, but I told him you wouldn't take offense to having someone say so."

Sharon returns the smile and motions for them to sit. "Not at all. Thanks. Just a guess, but I'd say you're not from around here."

"You see, Dennis, smart too." He continues, directing his words at Sharon. "We're just a couple 'a poor Aussies lookin' for some drinkin' mates."

Lynn is quick to offer her own welcome. "Join us and have a drink."

"No offense, mates," explains George, "but we saw you were drinking lolly water and thought something a little more … well, *alcoholic* might be … appropriate?"

"I agree with you, but they're pretty tough on liquor on the beach," explains Sharon.

"Just what Dennis and I figured, so we thought we'd invite all of you to a pub for a few schooners, or if you'd rather, we could stop at a bottlo, pick up a little grog, and go to another beach and throw some hot dogs on a barbie. How does that sound?"

Sharon pops to her feet. "Best plan I've heard yet. Who's in?"

VII

IN 1851, TWENTY YEAR-OLD WILLIAM Bradbury, desperate for an adventure, left his father's small farm in Northern Ireland. Word was that gold had been discovered in Australia.

William joined a horde of prospectors who came from all parts of the world. By 1852 some 100,000 people had arrived in Australia suffering from gold fever. Most, including William, were unsuccessful and soon either left or looked for other work to survive.

William found work as a laborer in the coastal town of Townsville for several years before he was able to purchase a piece of land on which he built a small home. A marriage followed the next year, and the first of three sons was born a year later. In 1871 gold was discovered in Charters Towers, Queensland. William hurried to get in on the early success, becoming one of the first, though minor, investors in what was to become one of Australia's major gold rushes, producing an enormous fortune for many.

William's second son, Frank, did not share his father's drive to find gold. Instead, he had a keen interest in the land and raising livestock, which he sold to restaurants in nearby towns. His father, now comfortably wealthy, gave him enough money to get a large piece of land on which he could pursue his dream of raising cattle.

Frank, in turn, prospered, raised a large family, and increased his land holdings. On a trip to visit a friend in the township of Gunnedah, he fell in love with the fertile black soil plains of the Namoi Valley and soon made a deal to trade his holdings in Queensland for property in New South Wales. Until the time of his death at seventy-six in 1936, he and his only son, Benjamin, continued to increase the size of the ranch.

After his father's death, Benjamin decided to diversify his holdings. He reduced the size of his cattle herd and turned his attention to the growing of both wheat and cotton. Wheat was the most widely grown crop in the shire, and some of the best cotton in the world now came from the area.

Benjamin's son, George, was born in 1986, and as the only heir, learned the duties of running the ranch under the tutelage of his father. As was true in his father's case, George was born at home on the Bradbury Ranch, some twenty miles from the town of Gunnedah.

Each had learned from his parents not only how to work the 10,000-acre ranch, but also acquired a love of books as the parents of each carried on the family tradition of reading and discussing every evening after dinner.

Everything seemed to be going quite well, and the Bradbury Ranch continued to prosper and grow until a serious drought beginning in 2002 severely crippled a large part of Australia. A series of fires compounded their problems, and the drought continued through 2007, causing many farmers and cattlemen to sell their livestock and move off their farms or ranches.

Exceptionally bright and academically motivated, George had always desired the opportunity to both receive a university education and to broaden his horizons, so he was delighted when he received the opportunity to go to school in the United States, particularly since his best friend and school chum had an identical plan. Shortly after the turn of the century, George and Dennis enrolled at the University of California in Berkeley. George's announced major was Environmental Studies, and Dennis' long-range goal was the law.

Shortly after the Aussies witnessed the volleyball victory and invaded the celebration on the Santa Cruz beach, George and Sharon fell deeply in love. After graduation he returned to the ranch to help in its operation, while Sharon, at the insistence of her parents, remained to complete her studies. The separations were unbearable, and the trips back and forth were becoming increasingly tedious and expensive. They planned a wedding to take place three days after Sharon's graduation. Kristen and Paul reluctantly agreed. They were fond of George but were afraid of a possible future move to Australia, hence losing their daughter as they looked at it.

They honeymooned in Hawaii, and on their return took an apartment in Sausalito. George, giving in to pressure from his father-in-law, took a position in his firm to learn the computer industry. Against his own desire, but with his parents' blessing, George remained in the Bay Area so that he and his new wife could take part in the many opportunities available in such an exciting area.

Several vacations "down under" managed to keep George satisfied. Eric was born in February of 2012, and the couple began discussions concerning a permanent location to raise their family. They remained undecided until the death of George's father later that year, the result of a stroke. After that, their choice became clear. In the summer of 2012, they moved to what would become their permanent home, the ranch in Australia.

It was a good time for their move. They had both grown increasingly disenchanted with the failure of the American people to deal with the problems facing their society. The political turmoil, the quagmire in the Middle East, the failure to responsibly confront environmental challenges, the growing gap between economic classes, and the deterioration of moral values led them to seek a fresh beginning.

To their great joy, they found that the new life met their every need. For George, it enabled him to return to a familiar and comfortable environment while, at the same time, giving him the opportunity to fulfill his responsibility to carry on the Bradbury tradition. For Sharon, it provided a clear direction and challenge for her passionate and unconventional nature.

She immediately attempted to become as Australian as possible, doing everything she could to learn both local history and the history of her new nation. She avidly studied the customs, the traditions, and the odd speech patterns of those around her. On more than a few occasions, even George had to ask what she meant by an expression she had used.

Never one to tiptoe through a minefield, she directed her focus and energy on the issues that adversely affected her neighbors and her countrymen. She marched, she protested, she wrote articles, sent letters to the editor, supported the "save the planet" movement, and became an ardent member of the *Light Greens*.

Perhaps her most passionate pursuit was that of the simple life, one filled with an appreciation of the things most people never see because they never look. "Simplify but modernize" became her mantra. After considerable research and doing much of the work herself, she had solar panels installed and windmills built to make them totally energy independent. She designed a complete renovation of the home, not with the desire to beautify but to make it more functional while also serving as an architectural monument to a traditional past. Her boundless energy both amused and pleased George, and he was delighted to approve any project she suggested.

Brock was born in the summer of 2016, and shortly after his birth the practice of reading and discussing after dinner every night was reestablished in the Bradbury home. From the beginning, Brock, still in his crib, and four year-old Eric became accustomed, and even looked forward to, the nightly gathering. These interactive sessions, completely appropriate to the boys' ages and interests, grew in length and complexity as they matured.

George continued to enjoy his favorite sport of rugby by becoming a member of the Gunnedah Rugby Club, and Sharon quickly became the club champion at the Gunnedah Golf Club. The boys, appreciative witnesses of their parents' athletic prowess, soon pursued their own interests in a wide variety of sports. The Bradbury family thoroughly enjoyed their life in Australia.

On the evening of April 21, 2024, the family gathered in the living room to listen to Brock read his school report on the Australian bush fly.

"… the fertilized female looks for a place to lay her eggs. Cow shit is her favorite place—"

Sharon interrupts. "Don't you think cow 'dung' or cow 'pad' might be a more appropriate term to use in your report?" Eric and George share a quick smile.

"But you say shit," explains Brock. George nudges Eric and grins.

"Well … maybe I do, sometimes. But this is a report for your school."

"Okay. Which one?"

Sharon, having noticed Eric and George's secret look, turns the answer over to them. "I don't know. What do you two think?"

"How about 'dung'?" offers George.

"I kinda like 'shit,'" says Eric.

"Eric!" She turns back to Brock. "Go ahead, honey."

"After the female lays her eggs on the surface of the cow … dung … it takes just a few hours before the maggots hatch if the weather is really hot. Then they begin to dig into the cow … dung. They eat it as they go and try to get as far inside as they can to drink the watery mixture of bacteria and digested food."

Sharon reacts with a dramatic, "Ugh!"

Brock continues, "When the maggots are fully grown, they leave their home in the … dung. It's always at night, and after it leaves, it digs into the ground. If it is really hot, it can change into a fly within three days, but if it is cold, it can take as long as a couple of weeks. Bush flies usually do not go inside a house. If you see a fly inside, it is probably a housefly." He finishes and looks up to offer a proud smile in response to the applause he receives.

"What do they eat?" asks Eric.

"I don't know. Dad?"

"They want protein. You know, blood. That's why they're such pests at barbeques."

"How come they always try to get in our eyes?" quizzes Brock.

"They want the moisture in the corner," answers George.

Eric joins in the questioning, "How long do they live?"

"Only about a week or two—or less if I get out the flyswatter," responds George.

"Okay, guys, it's bedtime," says Sharon. "That's a great report, Brock."

George joins Sharon. "It sure was. Do you give it tomorrow?"

"Yeah. I think I'll add this stuff to my report."

"That reminds me, can you drive the boys to school?" asks George.

"Charley and I are going to work on the tractor before we do the plowing tomorrow."

"What's wrong with it?"

"I don't know. We have it up on blocks, trying to figure it out."

With the boys safely deposited at their school, Sharon uses the opportunity to do a little shopping at the super market. Her cell phone rings, and she retrieves it from her purse.

"Hello … oh, hi, Charley." Seconds later, the phone slips from her hand, landing on the floor a split second before she does.

VIII

THE SOUND OF THE FRONT door opening causes Kristen to drop the magazine she was reading, rise from the couch, and hurry to the front hall. Sharon barely acknowledges her mother's presence as she marches directly toward her father's office.

Kristen, in hot pursuit, asks, "How did it—"

"It was awful. They were so goddamned inflexible."

"Oh, honey, I'm sorry."

Just as Sharon arrives at the door to her father's office, it opens. Paul stands in the opening, searching Sharon's eyes for a clue to the outcome. "What happened?"

"Dad, what about my exception?"

"Adam Wilkerson's handling it," he explains. "He's the best. But this is tougher than we thought."

"It's pretty damned shitty that it took you this long to tell me!'

Paul looks at Kristen as he speaks. "Yeah, we should have talked to you about it earlier, but—"

Kristen interrupts. "Why are you so opposed to at least considering it?"

"Consider having Eric taken away? God, Mother!"

"But everyone says it's wonderful."

"I just listened to a line of bullshit from the guy who runs the place, and it all sounds pretty stupid to me. Maybe it works for people the way things are here, but we aren't from here, remember? We loved everything about the boys' school at home. I just hate that we have to go along with this change. Dad, would you get me an appointment with Mr. Wilkerson?"

The secretary opens the door for a nervous Sharon who enters the plush interior of the attorney's office. Adam Wilkerson, a distinguished man in his early sixties, rises from his seat behind his desk to greet her. He gives her a friendly peck on the cheek and invites her to sit.

"How are the boys? Margaret and I haven't seen them in years."

"They're fine."

"Your parents talk about them all the time. We'd love to see them."

"Mr. Wilkerson—"

"Adam, please. We've known each other since you were a little girl."

Sharon takes a deep breath before continuing. "Adam … please forgive me for not being more … well, cordial, but you see, I'm terribly worried about Eric. That's why I'm here. Dad said you were handling the matter."

Adam's informal manner slowly subsides. He sits back in his chair and assumes the role of legal counselor. "They made a no-exception rule three years ago. Sharon, I'm terribly sorry, but the request has been denied."

"Exactly what does that mean?"

"Eric will have to enter the program."

"No!"

"I wish I could help, but you haven't a chance. The State takes quite seriously its obligation to protect the best interests of the child."

"What about my rights as a parent?"

"Believe me, my dear, I've pursued every legal course of action available to us. I wouldn't hesitate a second to represent you in court if there was a chance."

The next day, after Kristen responds to a knock at their front door, she opens it to find two uniformed policemen standing in its opening.

"Afternoon, ma'am, I'm Officer Ignatius, and this is Officer Conroy. Here are our identifications." The two hold open their wallets with a badge showing. "Sorry to disturb you, but we're here to see Mrs. Sharon Bradbury."

"What's this all about?"

"If we may see Mrs. Bradbury, we'll explain it to her."

"She's upstairs, lying down. I'd hate to disturb her."

"I'm afraid that's necessary. Would you please?"

"All right." Kristen motions toward the living room. "If you'll wait in there, I'll let her know you're here."

The two officers take a few steps in the direction of the living room, and then turn and watch Kristen disappear up the stairs.

Fifteen minutes later, standing next to her front door, Kristen watches helplessly as Sharon is led away in handcuffs.

The next morning, Adam Wilkerson, Sharon, and her father stand before a judge in court. The judge addresses the three. "Mr. Wilkerson, it's very important that your client follow the law in this matter."

"Yes, Your Honor." replies Adam.

"Do you understand this, Mrs. Bradbury? To ignore a court order as you did is a serious offense. If it happens again—"

"But, Your Honor—"

Adam stops her. "Not now, Sharon. Thank you, Your Honor. We appreciate your consideration in the matter."

An hour later, accompanied by her father, Sharon enters through the Webber front door and immediately heads for the stairs leading to her bedroom. Kristen starts to speak, but Paul directs her to be silent.

With the emotional dam now broken, a sobbing Sharon enters her bedroom and throws herself on the bed. She buries her face in a pillow and remains this way for several minutes.

Cried out, she sits up, stands, and walks to the window. A sailboat in the bay draws her attention, and she watches it maneuver unusually close to the shore before her problem again takes center stage. A strange combination of anger, embarrassment, and fear leave her confused as to what to do next. Fight back? Punch that goddamned Thornberg in the nose? That's a lovely thought. Pack up their stuff and head straight for the airport. Coward's way out, maybe, but safe. And when did running away from a problem ever work in the past? Spend another awful night (or more?) in jail as Eric is carted away to end up behind bars?

Come on, Sharon, think logically. What would George do? Forget that, he's not here. It's your problem now. How can any rational human being take away someone's child? How can a society condone such a barbaric practice? Surely there must be an answer to all of this. But what? Where do I go to find it? Who can I talk to?

She looks at her reflection in the mirror and is shocked to see the degree to which her emotions have affected her appearance. She turns away and looks for anything that would offer relief. Her eyes light on the framed photographs sitting on her dresser. One by one, she runs her finger down the edge of each frame as she reaches back into her memory of the moment: Eric, fishing pole in hand, standing on the bank of their pond, smiling over his shoulder at the camera, with George and Brock waving at the camera in the background; Brock, on his sixth birthday, mugging for the camera as he sits in his new canoe wearing his new kiwi hat; a family portrait, George and Sharon in the middle, flanked by Eric and Brock; dinner at the ranch in Australia with Sharon's parents and George's mother, with everyone holding a glass of wine to toast the occasion; Sharon, George, Dennis, and Lynn enjoying sandwiches and soft drinks as they relax and sunbathe in their personal inflatable off the coast of Carmel.

Sharon smiles, picks up the last photograph, and eases into a chair. Images of the Monterey dive site come flooding back. The three divers (Sharon, George, and Dennis), wearing full SCUBA gear, weave in and out of a kelp forest. A group of sea lions pass overhead. One member of the group approaches to study the divers. The mammal watches them for several seconds before he decides to perform an intricate underwater ballet, deftly moving around and between the long strands of seaweed that flow with the current. Tired of this, the sea lion speeds directly at them, veers to one side, and disappears.

It's now a playful otter's turn to amuse the group. He maintains pace with them and appears to want to touch his new friends. Sharon reaches out to stroke the delightful creature only to have it dart away, then quickly return to continue the game. Suddenly it is gone for good.

A kaleidoscope of colorful fish and invertebrates provide a feast for the divers' eyes as they move along the bottom.

A sudden thought brings Sharon to her feet. She finds the picture of her wedding party and focuses on the smiling face of the man standing next to her new husband.

"Dennis!"

Sharon quickly moves to some boxes stacked near the bedroom wall. She finds what she's looking for, opens it, and pulls out an address book. She consults the book, turns to the A-phone with the command, "On, phone." Following this, she reads the numbers and sits on the bed waiting for the response.

"Mr. Hardin's office. May I help you?"

"Yes. May I speak to Mr. Hardin? Please tell him it's Sharon Bradbury ... thank you ... Dennis, hi! ... we're in Carmel with my parents ... yes, we're fine ... I know ... thanks ... no, I didn't expect you to ... yes ... I called because—because I need your help."

IX

SEATED AT A TABLE IN a small cocktail lounge, Sharon peels the last strip of label from her beer bottle as she completes her story. "So, that's about it."

Dennis is slow to respond. "Well, you've got yourself quite a problem."

"I really didn't expect you to come all the way from Chicago."

"I'm just sorry I didn't get down to see you two more often. You've certainly had your share of bad luck. The drought ... the fires ... then George."

"And now this damned DE."

"I know how you feel, but you haven't seen first hand the miracles it's working here."

"Oh, Jesus, Dennis, not you, too! Australia's not exactly a primitive wilderness."

"Of course not. But I think you forget how bad it was getting. Look, you have to understand what you're up against."

" I'm trying."

"Before they revoked your passport, you might just have gone back to keep Eric out of DE. Now, I don't know."

"So, what do I do?"

"I'm not in the best position to advise you 'cause I can't practice here. What about the attorney your dad retained?"

"About all he managed so far is to keep me out of jail. I have to appear in two days. But he's a dead end. To begin with, he's so damned conservative that he'd be scared to death to rock the boat. And from what I found out, he even represented DE in several cases a few years ago. He's just giving lip service to satisfy my parents. They're old friends."

"Well, I'll do everything I can. I'm sure I can help in some way."

"I just needed some advice from a friendly voice for a change. I couldn't ask you to take time away from Monica and the kids."

"Hey, she's used to being the wife of a lawyer."

"Maybe, but it's still not fair. "

"The way things are, I think I might just try to go home if I were you.

41

I'm pretty sure we could arrange that, although they're getting pretty nasty about a lot of things lately."

"I know that's the intelligent thing to do, but …"

"What?"

"My pigheaded notion that this is my country, too. I can't help but believe they're trampling all over my rights, and I haven't done anything but feel sorry for myself up to now. It's about time I stopped. Dammit, Dennis, I'm a fighter. Have been all my life for the things I think are worth fighting for."

"You know, ever since you called, one name has been running through my mind: Patrick O'Conner. I was in two of his classes at law school. Later, we became pretty good friends. Before he taught, he'd been involved in all kinds of fascinating cases. God, he was good! It's been ten years since I had any contact with him, but I'm sure I could locate him—if he's still alive. If I had an impossible case, he's the person I'd want on my side. What do you think?"

"Sure, why not?"

Dinner has ended, and everyone has moved to the enormous Webber game room that contains an entertainment system that would impress even the most discerning audiophile and videophile. At the moment all are gathered at "ringside" watching two fighters in the middle of the room, which has become a "ring." One is a heavily muscled, hulking brute that methodically stalks the other boxer: Eric. In every way the action seems real except that Eric, while no physical match for his opponent, does possess extraordinary boxing skills and a quickness that allow him to hold his own and even, as the round progresses, gain an advantage.

The bout is in the later stages, and both fighters, blood flowing from their mouths, are tired and sweaty. Suddenly, the frenzied manipulation of the controls by Eric matches the frenzied activity of the fighter in the ring.

Two rapid left hooks follow three, four, five sharp jabs. The beast stumbles back into the ropes attempting to protect himself from the onslaught, but it is to no avail. After two crashing right hands through the weakened defense, the brute crumples to one knee and then crashes to the canvas as Eric steps away.

All cheer, except for Sharon who has watched the contest dispassionately. The referee appears, counts to ten, and raises Eric's hand to signal victory.

Kristen stands and announces, "It's about time for the sunset. It should be a good one. Hurry up." She heads for the living room with everyone following.

As soon as she enters the living room, she says, "wide open." The curtains, already partially open, respond to her command and pull back completely to expose a gigantic picture window that provides a panoramic view of the coast. A slow transformation follows, with the window now becoming a magnification glass that zooms in on the water line on the horizon. Cirrocumulus clouds that resemble the scales of a fish reflect the red light of the setting sun. Truly a breathtaking vision for all except Sharon who hangs back, preoccupied.

Finally, she gives voice to her thoughts. "Mom, would you take care of the boys for a couple of days? Dennis and I are driving to Mendocino to talk to a friend of his—an attorney."

"Of course, sweetheart."

Later that night, with Brock asleep in the bed next to them, Sharon sits on the edge of Eric's bed. She tenderly strokes the hair back from his forehead. Aware of her mood, he allows it.

"Will you be okay?" she asks.

"Sure."

"You're not worried are you, honey?" Eric shakes his head in response. Sharon continues, "We're gonna' make everything okay. I promise you."

X

PATRICK SHANNON O'CONNOR WAS BORN in Hawaii on June 10, 1941. His Irish father, Sean, a native of Great Britain, had grown up in London. Patrick's mother, Nancy, the daughter of a prominent vintner from Sonoma, California, spent the summer after her high school graduation in London where she met Sean. They fell in love and were married in the fall of the following year. Sean was drafted into the British army in 1937 and served until 1939 when he received a medical discharge after breaking his arm falling out of a jeep. After his discharge, the couple moved to California where Sean went to work for Nancy's father. To his great consternation, almost immediately after he became an American citizen, he was drafted into the American army. He was stationed in Pearl Harbor and was one of the first servicemen killed in the Japanese sneak attack.

In January of 1942, Nancy and her seven month-old-child returned to California to live with her parents. She worked at her father's winery until she re-married in 1950. She and Patrick, now nine, moved to their new home in San Francisco. After Patrick graduated high school, he was admitted to Stanford University. He graduated at the top of his class and immediately chose to enter the Stanford Law School. After three years he had distinguished himself as the top scholar of the class of 1965.

Wooed by law firms throughout the country, he chose instead to start his own practice. When his mother asked why he made such a choice, he merely shrugged his shoulders and smiled. The truth was that it provided him with the freedom to keep flexible hours and to choose interesting cases, most of which fell into the realm of "impossible." His remarkable record of victories over a period of ten years became legendary.

Then one day in his mid-thirties, while attending a Stanford basketball game, he found himself seated next to the most beautiful and interesting woman he had ever met. His keen intellect and masterful vocabulary deserted him completely. He felt like a babbling, pimply-faced freshman in high school trying to impress the senior homecoming queen. Fortunately for him, Eileen found him "charming" and agreed to have dinner with him after he called the next day. Thus began a storybook love affair. From the day they were married three months later until her untimely death, they remained deeply in love.

In 1981 he joined a law firm in the Bay Area mainly to give him more free time to spend with his beloved "Leenie." Then, in 1990 he accepted a professorship at the Stanford Law School. During the next twenty-two years, literally hundreds of law students there listed Professor O'Connor as the person in their life they most admired.

Eileen's sudden death in 2012 left him totally devastated. He resigned almost immediately and retreated to their summer home in Mendocino where he became almost totally reclusive.

Sharon and Dennis, driving slowly along a winding road in the country, enjoy the picturesque countryside. Rolling hillsides planted in grape vines are bordered by giant redwoods through which old animal trails may be seen. The car comes to a stop at an intersection.

Sharon, the navigator, points. "There it is. Sunset Lane." Dennis directs the car down the road.

Sharon continues to give directions. "GPS says we're about there. Okay. Now—a quarter mile. On the right."

As the car rounds a turn, a beautifully situated vineyard about two acres in size appears. After they pass the vineyard, they come upon a house. The sun, peeking through the sycamores that surround the house, gives it a mottled appearance. Its architectural design clearly dates it, but in its setting is truly charming.

In front of the house, two men, facing one another, are in the midst of a heated argument. Dennis pulls the car to the side of the road. He gets out and takes a few steps toward the two. He stops and stands watching with a smile on his face. The red-faced older man gesticulates wildly.

"How in the hell am I supposed to know that?"

The other man, forty years his junior, struggles to maintain his composure. "I dunno'. It's the goddamned code!"

"Screw the code! I've been taking water out of that well since before you were born."

"Well, laws change."

"Bullshit! People change!"

"Shit, I'm not going to waste my time trying to talk sense to you. Get your license and install the meter, or we'll cement it over."

With that, the younger man turns and retreats to his pick-up. The older man glares at his opponent as the vehicle wheels around and screeches away.

Dennis, still some distance away, calls out, "Patrick."

Patrick looks up and shades his eyes as he looks in Dennis' direction. He walks toward him.

"What the hell do you want?"

Dennis does not answer until Patrick draws close. "It's Dennis Hardin. From law school."

Patrick stops and looks at Dennis for several seconds. Slowly, the recognition registers. "Dennis Hardin! You crazy Aussie son-of-a-bitch. How the hell are you?"

"Jesus, I wasn't sure you'd remember me."

"How in God's name could I forget a wild bastard like you? I'm not senile yet."

"It's been more than fifteen years."

"Yeah. Where the hell you been?"

Under the grape-covered arbor of Patrick's patio, an open bottle of sparkling wine and three flutes rest on the table in front of the two guests and their host. Patrick is in the process of filling the flutes as he speaks. "So, Sharon, how did you get mixed up with a reprobate like this?"

Dennis is quick to explain. "Sharon's husband and I were best friends. We came to the States together. I was the best man at their wedding. He was just killed in an accident."

"Oh, Jesus! Here I am going on like an idiot. I'm really sorry."

"We're the ones who owe you an apology," explains Sharon, "intruding on you like this."

"Nonsense. Someone's gotta' help me drink this stuff."

Two sheriff's deputies, each with a hand on Eric's shoulder, lead him to the waiting patrol car in front of the Webber home. Kristen, hand over her mouth, watches helplessly from her front porch.

As the deputies and their charge approach the car, Brock and two of his new buddies arrive on their bikes. Brock, seeing his brother in peril, reacts instantly. He drops his bike, sprints toward the abductors, and dives headlong into one of the deputies, almost knocking him off his feet.

The other deputy grabs Brock and pulls him away from his partner. A subdued smile plays across his face as he motions for Kristen to come to their aid.

Moments later, with Kristen's arms clamped around Brock, Eric looks back at the pair as he gets in the car. The last thing he sees is Brock's tear-stained face before he turns and faces forward.

Patrick, his Irish spirit now fully aroused, is busy venting his spleen. "Hell, the fight was half the fun! Not like it is now. Now everything is so goddamned devoid of guts—of a willingness to fight for the things we value."

Dennis smiles and looks at Sharon to see her reaction. "It's nice to see you haven't changed from the law professor I admired. Do you remember how some of us smart-ass students used to call you 'Don' for short cause you only had fun when you were tilting after windmills?"

"We did have some fun, didn't we? Now about all I tilt is one of these." He picks up his glass and drains it. While he refills the three flutes, he turns his attention to Sharon. "Let's get back to your problems with D.E."

"That's why we're here," answers Sharon.

"On the surface I'd say you have a good argument. But, there are lots of things to consider and lots of problems to face. And I'm sure you know going in you're up against a pretty powerful bunch. A few years ago I'd have been licking my chops, but I'm afraid it requires a mind a little sharper than mine now."

Dennis is quick to disagree. "I doubt that. I've never seen—" The sound of the phone inside interrupts him.

"Damn!" exclaims Patrick.

He sets down his flute and disappears inside.

Sharon smiles and looks at Dennis. "He's certainly everything you said he was. And God, it's so refreshing to talk to someone who doesn't treat DE as something sacred."

"I don't think anything is sacred to Patrick—unless it's this stuff we're drinking."

"I'd say it sounded … encouraging?" says Sharon.

"Well, he didn't discourage you."

Just then, the door opens and Patrick steps outside.

"It's for you, Sharon. It's your mother. Said she couldn't reach you on your cell phone."

"I left it in the car. What could my mother want?" Sharon rises and goes inside.

"Something wrong?" asks Dennis.

"She didn't say." Patrick picks up his flute.

"This has been great for her. She's been so depressed about the thought of losing her boy."

"I hope she hasn't misinterpreted my assault on the establishment as encouragement to take on DE."

"She probably has. But that's okay. It's what she needed."

Sharon opens the door and stands looking out and past the two men. It is several seconds before she speaks. "They took Eric."

"Who?" Dennis asks.

"The Sheriff. Just came and ... took him."

Everyone remains silent as they search for the right words to express their feelings. Finally, Patrick rises, lifts his glass, drains its contents, and announces, "Give me ten minutes to throw some things into a bag. We can be there before dark."

XI

THE SUN IS JUST SINKING into the Pacific Ocean as Dr. Thornberg finishes his explanation. He is seated at his desk in his office as Patrick and Sharon, visibly shaken, stand facing him across the desk.

"Several attempts were made to make Mrs. Bradbury aware of the law. She chose to ignore it, and we merely followed established procedure."

Patrick, his face flushed, is quick to respond. "Established procedure doesn't include kidnapping someone's child! Your arrogance is appalling."

"The law is quite clear in this matter, Mr. O'Connor."

"The injunction I get tomorrow will be equally clear. You could save us all a lot of trouble by releasing the boy right now."

"Your naiveté is amusing. Get your injunction—if you can—and we'll settle this in court."

"Fine, I'll do just that."

Sharon's anger at last boils over. "You bloody jackass! I'll—"

Patrick quickly takes Sharon's arm and moves her toward the door. Before they reach it, Thornberg stops them with, "Oh, Mrs. Bradbury, would you please take this package?"

Fists clenched, she turns to face him. "What is it?"

"A Parents Guide to DE."

Patrick answers before Sharon can form her words. "What's the point? Eric won't be here that long."

"That's … something to be decided later," offers the smiling Thornberg. "In the meantime, we need to begin our programming for his attitude development."

Neither Patrick nor Sharon respond. Thornberg continues.

"Attitude Development, Mrs. Bradbury, includes such things as social, political, and religious affiliations. Literary and musical tastes. Preferences for leisure time activities. And much more."

Dumbfounded, Sharon can only muster a weak protest, "You don't mean… the parents make all those choices? My God!"

"That's where the schools started to break down. Parents could no longer trust them to establish and fortify values and beliefs."

"Those were things," Patrick points out, "our generation created for ourselves."

"Times have changed, Mr. O'Connor."

"Bullshit! People have changed!"

Sharon grabs the packet, and the two leave the office.

Outside, Sharon and Patrick walk quickly to the car in which Dennis is seated. He sees them coming, jumps out, and opens the door for Sharon. She angrily throws the packet into the back seat and climbs in.

"What happened?" asks Dennis.

"The son-of-a-bitch didn't bat an eye," answers Sharon.

Patrick explains, "I expected as much. But we had to fire an opening shot, Goddammit, to let him know the war has begun!"

XII

SHARON AND BROCK ENJOY A walk together on the beach.
  "Mom."
  "What, sweetheart?"
  "I miss Eric."
  "So do I. But we're working to get him back."
  "Why does he have to go there?"
  "It's just the way they do things here."
  "Will I have to go?"
  "No. You will not!"
  "That's what you said about Eric."
  The two continue their walk in silence. A large group of seagulls on the beach dead ahead captures Brock's attention. He crouches low and gradually increases his pace toward them. As soon as the first nervous bird takes flight, it becomes Brock's signal to break into a full sprint directly toward the middle of the bunch. With arms waving wildly, he completely clears the beach of their presence. With a look of satisfaction he jogs back to join his mother. Her smile is soon replaced with a look of concern as they quietly continue their walk. Finally:
  "Your new home's a little confusing, isn't it?"
  "Kinda."

Their walk now finished, Sharon and Brock return to the Webber home and find Dennis and Patrick deep in conversation in the patio behind the house. When the two men see Sharon and Brock, they both rise to greet them.
  Sharon is the first to speak. "How'd it go?"
  "About what we expected," says Dennis.
  Patrick adds, "Our injunction to return Eric was rejected. But, we do have a court date in a little over two months. Good timing. Good situation. Things are ... good."

"Then why do I get the feeling that the house has just fallen down?"

Dennis pulls out a chair and invites her to sit. "No! We were just working out our schedules. I have to go back … my practice … my family. But I'll be back for the trial."

"Dennis, of course. I understand that. I've asked too much already."

Patrick offers his own explanation. "And I'll be gone, too—for a while. I have a lot to do back at home. Dennis and I will be in touch daily. We're worried about you. Will you be all right?"

Dennis continues an expression of their concern. "It might be kinda' tough on you being here … with Eric there."

"Don't worry about me. I'll be fine." With that, she slumps into the chair and offers a courageous smile.

Midnight in the Monterey Peninsula Academe Integral is much different than one would expect. In contrast to the cold fog that hangs over a quiet Monterey night outside, the classrooms, in full operation, hum with activity. In room 306, ten cubicles adjacent to one another rotate 180 degrees. When they come to a stop, they tilt forward to an upright position, and their fronts slowly rise. In a semi-trance, the occupant of each steps out and stands waiting. Eric is one of them. All are dressed the same—white pull-over top, mid-thigh length shorts, and "hospital slippers."

A muffled bell sounds, and the children dutifully form a line. It sounds again, and they move toward the ten utility rooms. Each child stops in front of the door leading to an individual room and faces it. The doors open in unison, and the children enter.

Inside the small room are a toilet, a shower, and a table. Eric sits at the table on which rests a tray containing four "squares" of food, each a different color, and a plastic bottle of a bright-red liquid. As he does so, a pleasant voice from the speaker above directs his activity.

"Now, please take the yellow portion … chew slowly and carefully … that's right … isn't it tasty!"

As is true of all the children, Eric continues to do as instructed with no sign of emotion or pleasure. After the meal has been completed, the water in the shower begins to flow. A different voice directs the next activity.

"Now, please remove all your clothes … place them in the basket next to the table … open the shower door, and step inside … now close the door.

"Doesn't the nice warm water feel good? … be sure to wash thoroughly … use lots of soap … get all parts … don't forget the toes … doesn't this feel good!"

Later, with the shower now finished and the children thoroughly dried, another voice finishes the instructions.

"Your nice, fresh clothes are on the shelf … first, your pants … that's good … now your top … and now your slippers … don't your clean, fresh clothes feel and smell lovely?"

Another muffled bell sounds, the doors open, and the children step out and move to a position in front of their pod. Again, the bell sounds, and the front rises. All—except Eric—step inside. As the doors close and the pods begin to rotate, Eric sneaks in the direction of the door.

A few minutes later, Eric, flanked by a worker on one side and a guard on the other, enters the room and walks toward his cubicle.

XIII

SNUGGLED SAFELY INTO A PRIVATE spot on a cliff above the beach, the funky little beach house retains a charm it has held for more than forty years. Lynn sits on the small deck, reading. She looks up, sees the two visitors begin their approach up the stairs from the beach. She smiles, waves, and stands to greet them. "Sharon!"

Later, the two nurse glasses of Chardonnay as they watch Brock dig a protective moat around a castle on the beach below. Their conversation has taken a serious turn.

Sharon speaks. "Everyone I talk to has nothing but good things to say about it. You're the first person who isn't just gushing about how wonderful it is."

"I hate what it's doing to the kids."

"So, you have some in your classes?"

"That's all I have!"

"And ... you're not happy with them?"

"Happy?" Lynn reaches into the ice bucket, grabs the bottle, and fills their glasses. "Maybe I don't know what it takes to make a teacher happy. My complaints seem silly to damn near everybody."

"What are they?"

"Okay." Proceeding very slowly, as though searching for the right words to explain herself, Lynn looks directly into Sharon's eyes. "They're ... perfect, and I can't stand it." Sharon's blank stare merely heightens Lynn's intensity. "They're so full of facts that there's no room for questions. I teach *Correlation of the Arts*, remember? All I ever see from them is imitation. There's no creativity. No new ideas in any of their music, their art, their literature. They challenge nothing. They're devoid of any kind of vision. I see no desire in them to search for ... the truth ... for change ... in anything. I find it very depressing."

"I'm surprised. Do any of the other teachers agree?"

"Oh, a few in my department, but we're generally considered the whackos. The teachers in Math, Science, History—almost everyone else—love them.

They couldn't be better prepared in those disciplines. We've pretty much given up trying to get them to … let me give you an example of what I mean. Follow me."

Sharon looks at Brock below still building his sand castle before she follows Lynn inside the house. She watches her rummage around in a corner of her office. Lynn selects three photographs of oil paintings. She turns and hands one to Sharon.

"Look at this!"

Sharon takes it, studies it for a few seconds, and announces: "I like it. Van Gogh, isn't it?"

"No. Look at the name at the bottom. Marsha McClelland."

Lynn hands her another. Sharon offers a weak smile before offering her response. "I'm at a bit of a disadvantage here. Impressionist, right? Manet … Monet?"

"Manet is who you're thinking of. But it's an 'original' Henry Stewart. Another of our students. One more."

Lynn hands her the final photograph. Now getting the point, Sharon confidently states, "This is not a real Picasso."

"Bingo. You can see what's happening. It's all the same: formula … derivative. Technically terrific, but it's been done!"

"I don't understand."

"Neither do I."

"What's happened?"

"I wish I knew. I think it may be that the students revel in the way things are now. It's like their creative juices have dried up. Every form of artistic expression—their ideas, their literature, their music—lacks fire, wit, imagination …"

"How does this—" Sharon, suddenly aware of Brock's presence, directs her full attention to him. "How you doin', sweetheart?"

"Can I go in the water, Mom?"

"Sure, honey." Sharon seeks Lynn's approval. "Can we sit down by the water, so I can keep an eye on him?"

"Of course."

Sharon directs a loving pat on his bottom. "You lead and we'll follow." With that, Brock heads back to the stairs leading to the beach.

"I've been so wrapped up in Eric's problem that I'm afraid I've not spent much time with him. I've been promising him a trip to The City."

"Well, you sure wouldn't want to be there now. The diaper dandies have taken it over." Seeing Sharon's quizzical look, she adds an explanation. "The Nationalists. The party of our youth!"

A bank of TV cameras, a single spotlight, and a convention center full of youthful delegates focus on Helena Conniff as she stands before them at center stage. An extremely attractive woman in her mid-forties, Helena appears strangely out of place at such an event. The curly blonde hair framing her flashing eyes and sensuous mouth seem far more appropriate to a sound stage on a Hollywood set. Her voice, however, clearly combines the elegance of royalty and the passion of an evangelist as she concludes her speech to a capacity crowd at the Nationalists' Convention.

"And so, fellow Nationalists, I am proud to serve as your standard bearer as we prepare to embark on our journey into greatness. I accept your nomination for the office of the President of the United States!"

The celebration floodgates burst with a gush of cheers, balloons, confetti, lights, and music.

XIV

KRISTEN, SEATED AT THE KITCHEN table, sips from her glass of wine as Sharon prepares dinner. Next to Sharon's purse on the table is the *Parents' Guide to DE*. Curious, Kristen picks it up and thumbs through it.

"Where did you get this?"

"What? Oh, Thornbutt gave it to us when Patrick and I went to his office."

"What's it all about?" asks Kristen.

"I don't know."

"So, you haven't read it?"

"No."

"Aren't you even curious?"

"No."

Her own curiosity now stimulated, Kristen focuses more intently on its contents as she continues to skim the pages. Somewhere near the middle of the booklet, she stops and reads silently for several seconds before announcing, "This is interesting."

"What?"

"This part titled, *Attitude Development*. There's a section on almost everything: *Leisure Activity Preferences—Team Sport Affiliations—College Choice—Professions—Languages—Religion—Musical Tastes—Political Views* ... and on and on. Apparently you're supposed to select your preferences, areas of emphasis, amount of time devoted to its establishment—and lots more. How interesting!"

"My God, Mother. I think it's disgusting!"

"Well, it does seem only natural that the parents would—"

"Want to make all the choices for their kids? Make them carbon copies of themselves?"

"It's not as weird as you make it sound."

"All right, take us for example. We're about as different as two people can be."

"Nonsense."

57

"Oh? Religion. Politics. Immigration policy. Ecology. Hell, where do I stop?" Sharon pauses as she lightens up a bit. "You're nuts about the Golden Bears, when we all know Stanford rules."

"Well, now—"

"I'm not finished. But really, you like TV, and almost never read. I love to read. I love to swim. I can't remember the last time you got wet. You love big parties and being around lots of people. My idea of fun is a quiet night in front of the fire with the family. You have to have every new gadget they dream up. I think they're all totally unnecessary and a waste of money. For God's sake, you don't even like anchovies on your pizza! The point is, we're all individuals, and we should have the right to make our own choices."

Sharon smiles, confident that she's made her point, slips off her apron, and drops it on the booklet as she leaves the kitchen.

"Anchovies on pizza—ridiculous," mutters Kristen just loud enough for Sharon to hear.

Sharon stands watching a receptionist in the central office as he views the computer screen on his desk. "Your son is in Wing D, Level 3, Room 306, Mrs. Bradbury. You may use that elevator there."

As Sharon steps out of the elevator on the third floor, she looks around for signs of human activity. Nothing. No laughter. No hushed voices sharing little intimacies. No students hurrying to class or on their way to the bathroom. Nothing. The quiet is irritatingly incongruous with her picture of a hallway in the schools with which she is familiar. The walls, even, are depressingly sterile. No artwork. No posters soliciting votes for upcoming school elections. No announcements of games, dances, plays, club meetings. Lost in her thoughts, she does not notice an attendant's approach.

"May I help you?"

"Oh. Well, yes. Room … 306, please."

The attendant points to a door no more than twenty feet down the hall, then turns and disappears. Slightly embarrassed, Sharon quickly moves to the door indicated. She looks left and right before she gently turns the handle and slowly pushes open the door.

The room is much like the one Sharon was in earlier, and the cubicles are arranged in a similar alignment. Apparently only one person is present. Seated at the control panel reading is a surprisingly young-looking individual who has the scrubbed, clean-cut look of an "All-American" boy. As soon as Sharon closes the door, he puts down his book and looks up.

"Hi."

"Hello."

"May I ask whom you're here to watch?"

Sharon eyes him suspiciously before she responds. "Bradbury … Eric Bradbury."

The young man looks at the chart posted near the control panel. His eyebrows rise, and he sneaks a peek at Sharon before he speaks. "Okay. Number twenty-two. Right over there. There are some seats in front. Let me switch on the screen for you." He touches a button, and the screen on the wall is activated. It is a lesson in *Civics* but is projected at a pace that is difficult for Sharon to follow.

"This is what your son is working on. He's at level two. That's good for a "Newt." Sharon's non-response leads to an explanation: "Newt—a Newcomer."

Sharon now carefully studies Eric's cubicle. An "X" in red is posted on its front.

"Is this your first visit, Mrs. Bradbury?"

"Yes."

"He's fine in there … really."

"What's that 'X' for? None of the others have it."

"I think … he must have had a little … trouble at first."

"What kind of trouble?"

"I really don't know. Probably some kind of adjustment problem."

"There's no record of what the problem was?"

"No. I'm sure it wasn't serious."

After a pause, Sharon continues. "What's level two?"

"Each student learns in accordance to his or her own ability. He'll be a level five in no time. Here, let me give you a look." He flicks a switch, and the information on the screen accelerates to a point that is impossible to follow. After a couple of seconds he switches it off.

"Level five. Kinda' difficult, huh?"

"No offense, but you look like a bit of a newt yourself."

The young man laughs. "Yeah, I guess I am. I graduated just a couple of years ago. Been working here ever since. My name's Robert."

"You … went through all of this, Robert?"

"Sure. Pretty soon I'll be ready to do some of the programming."

"Did you … like it?"

"It's great! Would you like to see a text of the lesson, Mrs. Bradbury?"

"Yes, I think I would."

Robert goes to a file cabinet, opens a drawer, and pulls out a booklet. He returns and hands it to Sharon.

Sharon looks at it for several seconds before, "Do many parents come to watch?"

"Not a lot. But some do, sure. Usually on the weekends. Saturday morning and Sunday afternoons are pretty popular. Actually, you can come anytime, night or day."

"Is there some kind of schedule my son follows?"

Robert laughs. "Of course. Order is all-important. We look to our leaders to show us the way. Let me show you."

Robert turns to the computer, touches several keys, and then faces the printer. After a couple of seconds, a printout appears.

"Here you are. This is his hourly schedule for the rest of the week. Let me know if you have any questions."

Sharon takes the schedule and studies it very carefully.

"If I understand this correctly, he has ... let's see ... one, two, three, four, five, six, seven, eight—God, how many classes does he have today?"

"Let's see ... he has ten in this twenty-four-hour period. The asterisk indicates his 'classes' as you call them. This is a fairly limited schedule because it allows time for the basic program-conditioning that usually takes a month or so. Those are underlined. And he, of course, eats twice, exercises, and deep sleeps."

"I don't even see sleep here," says Sharon.

"Oh, that's 'Sopor.' Much more beneficial than ordinary sleep. At this stage he gets six hours. As he becomes more conditioned, he'll need less."

"Six hours! For a kid who usually needs at least nine?"

"Well, there's sleep, and then there's sleep. Sleep for most people is not very efficient."

"What about the need to dream?"

"That's all taken care of. I don't understand exactly how it works, but I do know that all that's needed is provided. You can talk—"

"He eats in there? Goes to the bathroom in there?"

Fully enjoying Sharon's naiveté, Robert laughs. "You're not kidding about this being your first time, are you? Here, let me show you."

He beckons Sharon to follow. They slide between two of the cubicles and come upon a row of "utility" rooms located behind the modules. An attendant is at work cleaning the area around the rooms.

"See," Robert explains, "here is where the students eat, shower, go to the bathroom."

"But they're so small!"

"They're alone, so actually there's lots of room in there."

"They even eat alone?"

"Well, sure. All the students stay in the 'programmed condition.' The schedule rotation keeps the rooms in use all the time. They're being used right now. Otherwise, I'd show you what they're like. Of course, they're cleaned"— a buzzer on the control panel interrupts him. "Excuse me for a minute, please."

The two return to the central area. Robert pushes a number of buttons on the control panel and then turns to the computer and hits several keys as directed by a chart he holds. After about thirty seconds Robert completes his task and turns back to Sharon who has been looking more closely at Eric's module. Eric may be seen from the waist down.

Robert turns his attention to Sharon. "There's a very detailed description and analysis of all the programs. Didn't you get a copy?"

"No."

"That's strange. All our parents are kept very well informed about everything that happens."

"Maybe it's not so mysterious. I haven't returned the ... 'Attitude Development' worksheet—or whatever it's called."

"Oh, well then that accounts for the blank space you see there ... about halfway down the sheet. Without that information it's impossible for the programmers to know what to input."

"It's supposed to create interests? Tastes?" asks Sharon.

"That, and a lot more."

"That's crazy!"

"Why?"

"What about making choices for yourself?"

"We get an opportunity for input. For example, I made my own decision about my profession. The graduate school I wanted to attend. The institutes I want to join. My political party. Social activities. Scientific projects I support. And lots more."

Sharon turns away and rolls her eyes in disgust.

Robert continues, "Order is the most important thing."

XV

SEATED AT A TABLE IN the elegant dining room of a private club, three men enjoy their drinks while waiting for lunch. Two of them, Donald Bartleby and Judge Lungren, both in their mid-sixties, and obviously professional men of considerable stature, nurse a martini, while the third man, known to the other two only as "Mr. Smith," sucks on a beer still in the bottle. Flecks of white foam, picturesquely harbored in his bushy, black mustache, serve as a source of unspoken amusement for his companions. Though Mr. Smith's crude manners and speech are in marked contrast to the learned sophistication of his tablemates, they both focus their full attention to what he is saying.

"This Bradbury dame, you'll be able to handle her?"

Bartleby is quick to respond. "Nothing to it. We haven't seen any cases like this lately, but we went through lots at first, remember?"

"Yeah, and a number of them were sticky," adds Mr. Smith.

"That was a long time ago. It's very different today," explains Bartleby.

"Then how in hell has she gotten this far with it?" quizzes Smith.

"And just how would you," asks Judge Lungren, "propose we go about denying her a day in court?"

Bartleby weighs in, "Might we be a little too concerned about this whole affair?"

"Let her win, you're saying?" asks the judge.

"One mother and her child," answers Bartleby, "What's the big deal?"

Judge Lungren concurs. "I think you're right. Would it be so awful if she were permitted to keep her son at home, Mr. Smith?"

"If she can do it, why can't everyone else? It ain't gonna' happen."

The judge takes a sip of his martini before he responds. "You really view it as that important?"

"Why do you think I'm here? Do I tell Dallas they should be worried about this?"

"That's not necessary," explains Bartleby, "It'll be over in no time. We're on top of it. She just got a little bad advice from someone on a crusade."

"Who?"

"An old law professor trying to relive his youth," says Bartleby.

"Should we take care of him?"

"No need. He's harmless."

Smith drains the remaining beer in the bottle and wipes his mustache on his sleeve. "You'd better be right."

In moderate traffic near Carmel, Patrick, dressed in work clothes, drives his '98 Ford Pickup manually. Thoroughly enjoying the scenic route, he looks around often and occasionally waves to other cars whose inhabitants smile as they pass. All the while his favorite tape keeps him company, and he sings along, song after song, with his favorite vocalist, Doris Day. His other companions, two suitcases and three cases of wine, are snuggled next to one another in the bed of the pick-up.

Paul, Kristen, Sharon, and Brock are seated at the dining room table in the Webber home having dinner. Patrick, their entertainment for the evening, is just concluding one of his many stories.

"… not sure whether the honking horns and their little gestures show their affection for me or my truck."

"Well, if you ask me, I'd say it's a mighty handsome little chariot you have," offers Sharon.

"It's my sweetheart. I use it every day. Almost never take my other cars out of the garage."

Paul raises his glass. "I certainly appreciate your cargo this trip. It's great."

The adults join Paul and lift their glasses in Patrick's direction.

"Glad you like it. I'm sure Dennis will be happy to help us. He gets here Saturday, right?"

"Yes."

"We've been in touch every day, but we've developed our approaches separately. I'm anxious to see what he has."

It is about midnight of the same evening. Patrick sits at the desk in the den making notes from an open book. Sharon enters with a drink in each hand. She sets one on the desk next to Patrick and sits on the couch.

"You've gotta take a break."

"I don't need much sleep," says Patrick.

"How's it going?"

"Honestly? Awful. This move of theirs to prosecute you really complicates things. It's pretty damn clever. Instead of being on the attack, we have to play defense."

"Don't worry about me."

"We have to. And they know it."

"What can they do to me?" asks Sharon.

"What more do you want? They've revoked your passport. You've been in jail. If we're not successful, you may be in prison. Don't kid yourself, they're not messing around."

"I just don't get it. Why are they so focused on my little situation? How can one mother and her kids be so important?"

"That's a hard thing to explain. You've got to understand the law and how it works. One block breaks down, and the whole tower crumbles."

"And we're the block?"

"Oh, you are now, but there are countless numbers who have come before you and will come after you."

"That's kinda depressing."

"Not for the lawyers. Remember the old coaching axiom? Win a few, lose a few? When do the lawyers lose? They just move on to another case."

"That's pretty cynical."

"You think so? Maybe you're right. Hey, this is getting a little too philosophical for my limited brain cells. Let's get back to your problem."

"How does it look for Eric?"

"Every argument I come up with is old stuff. All the precedents have been set."

"But isn't each case different?"

"The circumstances, perhaps. I thought the constitutional freedoms approach might work, but that was the earliest argument presented—and defeated. Even the ACLU supported DE."

"That's hard to believe," says Sharon.

"They took the side of the lower socio-economic groups. Actually fought in court for their rights to receive the benefits the program offered."

"What happened to freedom? Personal choice?"

"Depends on your perspective. At first, a lot of parents didn't want to be separated from their kids for any amount of time. But the argument was made that the schools did that anyway."

"But not like this! God, they take these kids away for four years!"

"Well, almost."

"Huh?"

"That was one concession they had to make. Parents insisted, and had their views upheld, that they had to have the kids a few times away from the program each year. A lot of experts believed it was basically because they needed to show them off. And the kids certainly did not disappoint. They were courteous, loving, smart as hell, healthy, well behaved—most important of all—and interested in everything in their parents' world. In short, a parent's dream. So, a week in the summer and a week at Christmas was negotiated and agreed upon. From what I gather, it played hell with the conditioning, but what could DE do?"

"Still, all that time away from your child."

"Studies showed that there were only a few minutes a day, before DE became established, when parents and kids even spoke to one another."

"You sound like that damned Thornbutt," says Sharon.

"You've going to hear all this in court. You'd better get used to it. You're challenging a sacred institution."

XVI

IT IS EARLY MORNING ON an almost deserted stretch of beach near the Webber home. A blanket of fog covers the coastline, making Sharon's solitary jogging routine even more lonely. Oblivious to her surroundings—lapping waves and groups of wary seagulls resting before their daily forage—Sharon's eyes focus on a void. The rhythmic sinking and sucking sound of her jogging shoes in the wet sand serves as a metronome for her troubled thoughts.

Ever so gradually the pace slows, as though the thought process required a total response from every part of her being. Finally, she stops, bends over, places her hands on her knees, and stares at the sand below.

With the fog brightening above, signaling its impending demise, Sharon now jogs along the road in front of the Webber home. She arrives at the walk leading to the house and turns to follow it.

Patrick and Dennis, busily writing, barely notice as Sharon enters the den. She watches them for a few seconds, and then wanders over to the window and stands looking out toward the ocean. Without looking around she asks, "Can I get you something?"

Both men mumble something like "no, thanks," but the tone of Sharon's voice causes Dennis to look up.

"Anything wrong?" asks Dennis.

"No."

"Have a good run?"

"Yeah."

"Nice day, huh?"

"Beautiful."

"Sharon, what's wrong?"

"I told you. Everything's swell. It's a beautiful day. The run was glorious. My room is clean. I don't have a goddamn thing to do but sit around watching someone do what I should be doing. That's my son in there! He's my responsibility!"

"Now, wait a—"

"No! I'm sick of waiting. I'm sick of sitting around feeling like a useless piece of ..."

Patrick, now aware of the problem, looks up and enters the fray. "Then get off your ass and do something! Find out as much as you can about DE. Know thine enemy!"

Patrick immediately returns to his work. Sharon turns and leaves the room without another word. Dennis watches her go.

"Kinda rough on her, weren't you?" asks Dennis.

Without looking up, Patrick concludes, "Of course I was."

Sharon, wearing dark glasses and sporting a new hairstyle in an attempt to achieve anonymity, sits apart from about a hundred other parents in the small auditorium. The eager guests generate a buzz of excitement as they informally discuss the upcoming meeting.

Dr. Helm, late forties, officious, but with something of the cheerleader in her, enters and walks to the lectern.

"Good morning! Welcome to the Alpha Group Parent Orientation. We have lots to cover, and our wonderful staff is anxious to answer all your questions and thoroughly prepare you for what's to come—a very exciting, fun-filled, and totally beneficial experience for your son or daughter. Before we give you a tour of our facilities, we'd like to have you see a short video titled, 'The Enchantment of Dormant Enhancement.' I hope you enjoy it."

The auditorium goes dark, and the parents turn their attention to the giant screen. An image of Dr. Thornberg appears. Speaking in an informal and friendly manner to the audience, he says, "Good morning, ladies and gentlemen. Welcome to the Monterey Peninsula Academe Integral. It's only natural that all of you sitting there share a degree of trepidation for what's in store for your child.

"With their permission I will use a couple sitting in our audience today to illustrate why we're here. Mr. and Mrs. Carter. May I call you Deb and Grant? I believe we may consider your experiences as somewhat typical and representative of those around you. Grant, you were born in San Jose in 1986, and Deb one year later in 1987 in Santa Cruz. Your son, Sean, is eleven. Grant, at the age of eleven in 1997, and Deb the next year, you two entered the sixth grade. Do you remember what it was like?"

Dr. Thornberg's image fades and is replaced by animated figures in a montage sequence. Though the situations are serious, the comic characters used to act out each activity provides an element of humor, eliciting a kind of nervous laughter from the parents throughout the auditorium.

- Gang members roam the halls of a school, and later, to everyone's amusement in the group, smear graffiti on the walls of a bathroom.
- Students walk through a metal detector as they enter a building. A bell sounds, and a uniformed policeman rushes to stop a small freckle-faced girl. She reaches into her backpack and produces a metal protractor. She smiles sheepishly.
- A shabbily dressed character openly exchanges a packet of drugs for money, while in the background a faculty member looks the other way.
- A rowdy class in session. The helpless teacher does his best to control an unruly few while the majority of the students impatiently wait for the instruction to resume.
- A teacher, totally boring, stands before his captive audience in the classroom. Head down, he reads from his notes as the children text or talk on their cell phones, sleep, or doodle. One student in the front row, trying to concentrate, finally gives up and lowers his head as he succumbs to the numbing droll.
- A somewhat chubby boy sitting in front of a video game grows chubbier by the second as he sits on the couch shoveling in chips and drinking a soda.
- A boy and girl talk on the school grounds. She has both her hands on her rounded stomach as he looks down at his tennis shoes.

The face of an animated character wearing the lab coat of a scientist now fills the screen. "Pretty rough time, huh? Hopefully you weren't forced to experience any of this personally, but you certainly know that's what it was like for a lot of kids you knew. Okay, so you survived, but it wasn't easy. You knew there had to be a better way." At this point a slow transition from the face of the animated character to that of a real person takes place as he continues to speak. "Fortunately, in 2006 a team of educators and scientists gathered to discuss both the well-being of our young people and the future of our society. They began to experiment with a number of different approaches. It took twelve years and the efforts of literally thousands of experts from every field imaginable to achieve their goal. In 2018 DE schools opened nationwide, and their record of success is nothing less than phenomenal. To tell the full story of DE, it would take far more time than any of you have, so let me at least summarize our major findings, goals, and achievements. First, we concluded that the negative influences in our young people's environment were far too difficult for them to overcome. It was finally decided that 'isolation' during these formative years was the only way to successfully eliminate these pressures. But it had to be an isolation that also provided the necessary positive reinforcements of established and agreed upon values and standards of behavior. So was born the DE module. Second, the recent discoveries made by scientists on the nature of sleep and its relationship to the conscious and sub-conscious mind led to the method we now employ that makes possible a maximum utilization of the brain's power while still providing the individual with the proper amount and type of sleep that is most beneficial. The problem of a failing educational system that was not meeting the academic needs of our youth was solved. Third, it was agreed that a broad range of experiences should be made possible that far surpassed what would be available otherwise. And, most importantly, these experiences should be shared with friends in an atmosphere that offered good, clean, safe fun. DE has become an expert at providing this. Inside the DE module a world of excitement exists. Fourth, health and safety concerns clearly needed to be addressed. With the aid of nutritionists, health practitioners, physical therapists, recreation leaders, and child psychologists, DE is accomplishing its goal of maintaining a healthy and happy child. No dangerous drugs. No driving accidents. No teenage pregnancies. No obesity. No bullying. Welcome to DE!"

In an enormous room that houses some hundred specialized exercise-pods, the parents are gathered around Dr. Palmer, a handsome, physically fit man in his early thirties. Sharon remains detached from the group, standing by herself several feet away from the tightly packed bunch.

Dr. Palmer, exuding an enthusiastic professionalism, explains, "We're very proud of the contribution we make to the health and well-being of these young people. Our motto, as you can see is"—he stops to point to a sign that hangs above the door—"'*A Sound Mind in a Sound Body.*' Our daily workout lasts fifty minutes and is individualized for each student. We concentrate on three general areas: cardio-vascular strength, which we achieve by means of aerobic training. The other two are muscle tone—or strength—and coordination. For these we use iso-kinetics and isometrics. Wander around. Get a closer look. Ask questions of any of the people on the floor. They're all experts in physiology and kinesiology."

Sharon raises her hand. Most of the parents turn to look at her as Dr. Palmer acknowledges her request. "Yes?"

"What's wrong with good, simple play for the kids? Fun!"

"Nothing! But most kids had simply stopped getting the exercise they needed. Before DE, their exercise had become a stroll in the mall or an afternoon sitting in front of a video game. We provide more good, safe, healthy activities for them in this one period than most kids managed in a whole week of play. And it's all supervised and modulated for their precise needs and capabilities. And, the *fun* you speak of is here. Let me show you."

Dr. Palmer attracts the attention of a technician near the control panel and points to a screen above. All the parents watch as a picture appears. Their view is of a path that winds through an idyllic countryside.

Dr. Palmer calls everyone's attention to the pods. "Look at the students." In the bottom half of the module the children's moving legs on a treadmill may be seen. "The kids are out for a nice run right now."

It is a spring afternoon, and as the parents follow the picture, the children cross a small bridge and move through a beautiful stand of trees.

"I see that today the activity is located in New England. Tomorrow it may be Yosemite—or on a beach in Hawaii—or through a Brazilian rain forest. Each day is different. And they learn about the area as they run. It lasts for about twenty-five minutes. Of course we set the proper pace for each individual child, and our many professionals on the floor monitor the vitals of each throughout the entire activity."

Accompanying the children during the run is a group of animated characters involved in all sorts of goofy antics. They jump, they summersault, they fall, they flap their arms and fly, they hide behind trees and jump out in an attempt to scare the kids. Pure *fun*.

"This is what they're seeing on their screens in the pods—and hearing." He motions to the technician, and the parents now hear the music and the sounds of nature that accompanies the picture.

The parents are more than interested, and their reactions are varied. Some laugh, point, clap hands in time to the music's beat, or even jog in place.

It is apparent that the demonstration is a complete success for all—except Sharon, whose face remains expressionless as she stands quietly watching with her arms crossed.

Slowly, the screen dims, the music fades, and the smiling parents gradually return to adulthood as they turn their attention to Dr. Palmer. "Now isn't that fun! Are there any other questions?"

"How many children can you work with here?" asks a parent.

"Well, let's see. There are one hundred stations. The room is used twenty-four hours a day. Allowing for cleaning and passing time for the students, we can handle about 3,000 per day. We have another area just like this on Level four. Quite a handful!"

Sharon's pent up emotions cause her tone of voice to rise as she asks, "You do this in the middle of the night?"

A patient and smiling Dr. Palmer replies, "There is no night—or day—for these youngsters. That's one of the advantages of DE, remember? Maximum use of the educational facilities. Other questions?" He pauses and looks at the crowd of faces. "Since there are no more questions, please walk around and see for yourself how we work with the children."

Dr. Helm, listening and watching in the background adds, "And as you do, please accept a little treat."

From a box being passed by one of the assistants, each person selects a plain, white package.

"Find out for yourself what a typical meal is like. A list of the contents is printed in the upper right corner. We passed out quite a variety of meals, so you may want to see what your neighbor has and make a trade."

Everyone tears open the package to reveal a small tray divided into four sections. The food in each section looks essentially the same: bland.

Sharon crinkles her nose and gives a little shudder.

Dr. Helm continues, "Don't be put off by what it looks like. Give it a try."

Sharon nibbles at a corner of one of the squares, and her expression slowly changes. She raises her eyebrows and then quickly looks around, fearing that someone may have observed her reaction. But the parents, pleased to have the opportunity to experience the various tastes, are delighted with the results and are oblivious to anything but their own gustatory pleasure.

"It's nutritionally balanced," explains Dr. Helm, " and, as I'm sure you agree, tastes great. Our nutritionists have worked long and hard to provide the perfectly balanced diet for a teenager."

With a look of defeat, Sharon replaces the half-eaten square, sets the tray on a table, and quietly heads for the exit.

In room 306, seated next to the master panel and busy with his paperwork, Robert does not notice Sharon enter. When he does, he stops work, smiles, offers a greeting, and watches her walk to a bench near Eric's cubicle and sit, staring blankly forward. The combination of her failure to acknowledge him and the look on her face is enough to cause Robert to swivel his chair in her direction and search for a reason for her behavior. Finally, he stands and moves to a cubicle near where she is seated and pretends to make some adjustment in the controls. Finally:

"Haven't seen you for a couple of days," says Robert.

Again, Sharon barely responds. She merely shrugs her shoulders.

Robert continues his attempt to capture her attention. "How are you?"

"Fine."

"You … don't—"

"I'm sorry. I'm just preoccupied."

"With the trial?" .

Finally, she turns and looks at him. "You know about the trial?"

"Sure. You're notorious around here. Nobody's taken on DE for a long time. When does it start?"

"Huh?"

"The trial. When does it start?"

"Monday … any thoughts?" asks Sharon with great curiosity.

"Oh, I can certainly understand it. Your feelings I mean. I know it must be very hard for a parent at first to be separated from the child for any period of time. You missed the parents' orientation. This would have helped a lot."

"I was just there—for as long as I could take it."

"It might help to understand what a special time this is for your son. It's exciting! I know I hated to leave the program. We went everywhere. We learned so much."

"I've never seen my son leave that damned box since this whole thing started."

"But the mind—it's what we see and feel that makes life so wonderful. I can't wait to spend time in my HiDEM each night."

"HiDEM?"

"Home Dormant Enhancement Module."

"What are you talking about? You have one of those things at home?"

"Of course. Life would be pretty dull without it. You should see the programs they have available now."

"You mean … you … still use it when you don't have to?" asks Sharon.

"It's great!"

"But that's … artificial! That's not real life."

"Real life, as you put it, isn't so special. I took a couple of real trips, and they were big disappointments. The travel time, the luggage, the delays, the expensive hotels, even the weather—all those inconveniences are just a waste of time. It's all right here, better than it can ever be in the real life you're talking about."

"God! How'd you get one?"

"I bought it. Most of the graduates I know have one. That's why I mentioned the orientation program. The parents get a chance to experience some of what we do, and they love it."

"Let me get this straight. You bought one of these things, and you keep it in your home—and you like it?" Robert nods and smiles condescendingly.

Sharon continues, "May I ask what it costs?"

"The price is immaterial, really. I have a good job here, so I can afford it. And there are thousands of programs that really don't cost very much at all. I can arrange for you to take the introductory course if you'd like."

"No, thanks."

Sharon abruptly rises and moves toward the door. Just before it closes behind her, and with her back to him, she throws Robert a quick wave of her hand.

XVII

SHARON, CARRYING ABOUT A DOZEN packets, bursts into the den where Patrick and Dennis are still at work. They are startled by her abrupt appearance. She almost shouts, "I got it!"

Both men are puzzled but slightly amused as well. Dennis is the first to react. "Is it contagious?"

"Seriously, I've got the angle we need."

His interest now peaked, Patrick asks, "For?"

"For the case! The argument you've been looking for."

"What is it?"

"I did what you suggested—remember your 'know thine enemy' crap? I know you were just trying to get rid of me, but I actually went to an orientation session for the parents. Today—this morning. I realized how little I really knew about DE, and I decided to find out more. Well, it was awful. I mean ... it all seemed so reasonable. I really tried to be objective about the whole thing. You know ... to avoid the 'poor mom whose son has been taken away from her' thing. All the mothers are in that position, and they seem to be okay with it, so I knew I had to find something else."

Dennis continues the probe. "And you found?"

"Nothing. Not at the orientation, at least. I was depressed, so I just left. I walked over to the room where they have Eric, and I talked to Robert. Have I told you about Robert? He's the young man who works there and who graduated from the program. We've become pretty good friends ... and he told me he has one. A module. You know, one of those things Eric's in. Called it a 'HiDEM.' Home Dormant Enhancement Module. Of his own! He'd bought it."

Dennis, amused but also interested, searches for the point. "So?"

"Well, don't you see? He's hooked! While most people are out living, he's home in that damned box. He needs it! Said life would be dull without it."

"You didn't know about them?"

"No, I didn't. At least I don't think I did. Maybe I've seen them advertised somewhere, but what does that have to do with anything?"

"Your parents have one," explains Dennis.

"They do?"

"Sure. Remember Eric's boxing match? That's one of the many things it can do."

Sharon falls quiet as Dennis continues. "Let's see, you want us to stand up in court and argue to get rid of them because they work so well? Everyone likes them, so they must be evil?"

"Damn it, Dennis, that's not what I'm saying at all!" says Sharon.

"No, but that's what everyone will hear. We can't—"

Patrick, listening carefully, interrupts. "Let's not be too hasty, Dennis. She just might have something here. I knew about them, but I guess I just never gave them a second thought. Go on, Sharon."

"DE should prepare kids for the rest of their lives. Right? If they spend even a part of their lives hidden away in some machine, well … it's wrong! H-D-E-M. Even Robert pronounced it 'HiDEM.' Hide 'em away from society so everything's nice and quiet for the rest of us."

Patrick rises and walks to the table, picks up one of the packets, and looks at it carefully before sharing his thought. "It does answer a question that's plagued me for a long time. These kids get this superior education and then are content to take relatively insignificant jobs. Jobs that can't possibly give them the kind of stimulation you'd think they'd have to have."

"That's true," adds Dennis. "I see it all the time, and I even worried at first that there wouldn't be anyone willing to take on any of the … well … less stimulating jobs we need to have done. I thought it might be a real problem, but—"

"But they seem more than content to lower their sights." Patrick continues as though searching for the lost piece to a puzzle. "What happened to the old fire in the belly? The ambition, the—"

"The machines!" Sharon gleefully pounds home her argument. "That's the problem. Why would they need anything else if the machines give them everything they want?"

Patrick looks at Dennis. "Any notion how widespread this is? How many kids spend excessive time in these … 'Hide-ems'?"

"I'm not sure. My kids are too young. I think they're pretty commonplace, though. I know a few kids, graduates from DE, who have them."

"Might help to know how many programs there are … who manufactures them … who profits from the sales. Who controls the program's contents."

Eager to be taken seriously, Sharon's enthusiasm boils over. "Hey! You don't need me here. We still have three days left before the trial. I'll do it."

Patrick gives Sharon his full attention. "Do what?"

"Find the answers to your questions!"

Patrick searches for something on the jacket of the packet he is holding and announces, "Produced in Dallas, Texas."

A small army of gardeners is in the midst of performing their artistry on the grounds of a magnificent estate. Near a large, three-story mansion, a man of about seventy, wearing common workingman's overalls, bends over a rose bed cutting off the spent roses. He is so intent on his task that he does not notice another man, dressed in an expensive business suit, emerge from the house and approach him.

Standing behind the focused worker, the man in the suit waits patiently to be noticed. Finally, he gently clears his throat to announce his presence. Annoyed by the interruption, the worker looks over his shoulder and growls, "What is it?"

"Trouble. San Francisco."

The worker sighs, removes a glove and pulls up the sleeve on his left arm to expose what looks like a large wristwatch. He pushes several buttons and waits. Several seconds later, a voice is heard from the tiny speaker.

"Yes, sir."

"What's the problem?"

"Some of the delegates are becoming difficult," answers the voice.

"Can't you handle it?"

"I'm not sure."

"What do you need?"

"A meeting."

"All right. Here. We'll let you know when."

The man in overalls punches a button, pulls down his sleeve, and slips the glove back on. He reaches out and delicately makes a cut before turning his head and finishing his business with the man in the suit. "Make the arrangements."

Sharon, with her activist juices flowing, has now thrown herself totally into her new challenge. At five in the morning, she is still on the computer searching for any and every negative view of DE dating back to its earliest inception. For the most part, her efforts have gone unrewarded. The huge majority of evidence has provided a rationale for the revolutionary program that most view as an intelligent answer to the burgeoning problems facing American education.

In fact, it has become clear that the volume of detracting views diminished significantly as the years passed. The mound of supporting evidence has grown in reverse proportion to that which attempted to detail its flaws. Several movements opposing DE did develop, but in almost every instance the membership consisted almost entirely of disgruntled parents who decried the loss of their children. Ironically, in a large number of cases the opposing parents actually found themselves among the new system's most ardent supporters after their children graduated.

To her credit as a zealous reformer, the contrary evidence has not deterred her desire to find the program's Achilles' heel. Pages of notes have been taken on almost every angle. Clearly, Dallas is the focal hub primarily because it is where the research center is located and the nation's largest H.D.E.M manufacturing plant is situated. Time and time again, the city's largest newspeak, *The Dallas Morning News*, served as the most current source of information on the research and development that was taking place within the DE community. Sharon's desire to speak directly to someone who might be objective leads her to decide on the *Dallas Morning News* as her best source.

Shortly after Sharon hits the "1" button on her cell phone and says, "Dallas Morning News," a pleasant female voice sounds. "Welcome to the Dallas News. How may we help you?"

"I'd like to speak to your … Managing Editor, I guess."

"May I ask the nature of your call?"

"I need clarification on a recent article on Dormant Enhancement that appeared in your paper."

"And your name please?"

"Sharon Bradbury."

"Is this a personal matter, or do you represent an organization?

"I … represent the Australian Education Association."

"Thank you. I'll see if Mr. Fields is available. Will you hold, please?"

"Yes."

Several seconds elapse. "Ms. Bradbury? My name is Richard Fields. What can I do for you?"

"As I told the young lady, I work for the Australian Education Association. I know how busy you must be, so I'll be brief. We've begun discussions on the feasibility of using Dormant Enhancement in our schools. I'm in your country to get as much information as possible on the program. We've reviewed the information DE provided at great length, but it was suggested that we should hear all sides. Since you're so close to the headquarters, I thought you might suggest things we've not thought of."

"As I'm sure you're aware, we've done hundreds of articles on DE through the years. You're more than welcome to look at our archives, and if we can clarify any points we'd be happy to try. Your timing on this is a bit unfortunate, however. We're still recovering from a recent personal problem that relates to what you're asking. Several months ago we began work on what was to be a series of articles on DE. One of our best reporters was given the assignment. He worked on it for a couple of months, and then he suddenly disappeared."

"Disappeared?"

"Yeah. Quite a mystery. We still don't know what happened to him. Left without a word to anyone. His wife hasn't heard a thing from him."

"Were the police ... "

"Of course, but they don't have a clue."

"That's terrible."

"We've had several feature stories on his disappearance. I mention it only because I'm sure he would have been helpful to you. We assigned someone else to the series, but she's barely begun. You're welcome to talk to her."

"Thank you. I'd appreciate that. Would tomorrow be convenient?" asks Sharon.

"I'm sure it would. I don't think she's here now, but I'll ask her to clear a little time on her schedule for you. Are you in Dallas?"

"No. I'm calling from Carmel."

"Carmel—California? Magnificent spot. Got a couple pretty nice golf courses there."

"Sure have. And I'm sure you've brought 'em to their knees."

"Well ... the scenery was awfully nice. What time would you like to call?"

"I'd like to speak to her in person. I have a flight scheduled. Maybe mid-afternoon, if it's all right with her? I'll call as soon as I arrive."

"Excellent. I'll make sure she's available."

Loading of the scheduled red eye flight to Dallas has begun. Sharon, in the company of about forty other passengers, enters the A320 Airbus and is greeted by a surprisingly perky flight attendant who offers a smile and a personal greeting to all. After locating her window seat, Sharon places a small carry-on under the seat in front of her and settles in to await the take-off.

With the plane in the air, her attention is momentarily drawn to the disappearing lights of a city below. A new attendant opens the compartment above Sharon, retrieves a pillow and a blanket, sets it on the empty seat next to her, and inquires, "May I get you something to drink?"

"Yes, please. Jack Daniel's, if you have it, on the rocks?"

"Of course. Anything else? Something to read?" asks the attendant.

"I don't think so."

The attendant disappears, and Sharon again stares out the window as she mentally reviews the list of activities she has planned upon arrival.

Later, her drink now finished, her head eases back against the pillow and her eyes slowly close. In a matter of seconds, Sharon's jaw relaxes, her mouth softens, and her breathing deepens. A passing attendant looks down at the sleeping passenger, picks up the empty glass, raises Sharon's tray, and turns off her overhead light.

In a dream state, a series of images appear, disappear, and re-appear in an altered form again and again. The subject of the sequence becomes clear—the victory celebration that continued in the pizza parlor after the volleyball game on the beach, with the celebrants seated around a table on which rest several pitchers of beer as they laugh and sing.

Suddenly, both of Sharon's eyes open. Then they partially close as she attempts to re-capture these pictures, this time with the aid of her conscious memory.

Sharon and George enjoy the friendly banter but have difficulty keeping their eyes off one another. Through hers, George is her Adonis—tall, broad-shouldered, and tanned with sandy-blonde hair above strikingly handsome and rugged features. Through his, she is Aphrodite—bronzed, shapely, and athletic, with a beautiful face that is not untouchably delicate, highlighted by flashing blue eyes and an infectious smile.

The friendly interlopers from Australia remain the focus of attention with Lynn taking the lead in the investigation. "Okay, it's time to hear your story."

Dennis gives her a look. "Our *story?*"

"Where are you from? What are you doing here?" quizzes Lynn.

George provides the perfect answer. "Enjoying a coldie with our new mates."

Lynn continues the probe. "Come on, you two weren't just 'wandering through,' I know."

"They got us, Den." George smiles and raises his hands in surrender. "You're not gonna' like this—we're your 'Golden Bear' cousins from across the Bay."

"Cal?" screams Lynn. "You guys go to Cal? Did you know this, Share?"

"Yeah," Sharon sheepishly admits. "George confessed a little while ago. I was afraid to tell you. But I thought we should take pity on them since we just got through kicking the hell outta them in the Big Game."

Lynn laughs, "Nice thought. We *are* the civilized school. Are you two players?"

"Nah," explains Dennis. "Football's too rough for us. We're rugby players—the gentlemen's sport."

"Rugby?" questions Lynn. "That's kinda brutal, isn't it?"

"Not really. Nothin' like beach volleyball," says George.

"Are you guys any good?"

"Not bad," says Dennis. "In the last seventeen years, Cal has won the National Championship sixteen times."

"Wow! Really? Are we any good in rugby, Share?"

Dennis beats her to an answer. "I think your team won a game a few years ago. St. Teresa's Girl's School, if I remember it right."

Lynn slaps his shoulder. "You still haven't answered my question. Where are you guys from?"

"Ever hear of Gunnedeh? No? New South Wales? How 'bout Australia?" Dennis continues through the sound of everyone's laughter. "Now we're graduates from that school whose butts you just kicked in football."

"Graduates? What are you going to do now?" asks Lynn.

"I'm getting ready to enter law school, and my mate, here, is about to go home to help his dad on their ranch."

Later, the group leaves the pizza parlor, as the sun is about to set in the West. Everyone, except Sharon, Lynn, George, and Dennis, discretely find a reason to be elsewhere, leaving the two couples alone. George is the first to offer a suggestion. "Ladies, I hope you don't have any plans we can't be a part of. We'd sure like to help you finish giving that trophy a proper christening."

"What's say, Lynn? Okay with you?"

"Sure."

"Is anyone hungry?" asks George. "I'm starved."

"How 'bout this?" offers Sharon, "There's a great restaurant—the *Crow's Nest*—in the Santa Cruz Yacht Harbor. Good food. Good drinks. Nice views. What do you think?"

"Sounds perfect to me. Our treat. Where are you ladies staying?"

"At my parents' in Carmel," replies Sharon. "What about you two?"

"We've got a mate in Monterey. We were on our way to see him to do a little SCUBA diving."

"That's perfect," says Sharon. "There's a great beach between the restaurant and there. How does a moonlight walk and a fire on the beach sound after we eat?"

"Super!"

Much later that night, the four sit around a small fire on the beach. A full moon above is reflected in the waves as they break on the shore.

"Tell us more," prods Sharon.

"More what?" asks George.

"Why Cal, all the way from Australia?"

"Why not? Great university—one of the best. We also fancied a crack at playing rugby. It's mighty big in our country, and Cal's the best."

"You see," adds Dennis, " George and I have been mates ever since we first met. We went all through school together, and we'd always figured why not university too? Almost didn't work for George. His dad owns a big ranch, and Australia's had some pretty rough times the last few years. This global warming thing hit us pretty hard. Droughts, fires, you name it."

"We go back several generations," explains George, "and each new one has taken over from the one before. My parents, just like theirs had for them, always insisted on my getting a good education before it was my turn. Then, with all these problems, I just couldn't leave 'em alone. Well, my dad wouldn't even listen to anything I said. Damn near threw me out of the house when it came time for me to go off to school. Said it had to be outside the country, too—otherwise I'd be coming home all the time to help out."

"How are they doing?" asks Sharon.

"Okay, but it's not been easy. They had to sell off some of the land, and they cut back on the size of the herd. My dad tried planting some crops to take advantage of the market, and that got hit pretty hard. But … things'll work out."

"George is planning to go back pretty soon. I'm staying to start law school." adds Dennis.

"Yeah, and everyone's worried about how he's gonna make it," says George. "I carried him all the way through Cal, you know. No chance he'd have made it own his own. Hell, he can't even cook … well … he can handle a dingo's breakfast." Dennis laughs.

"What's that?" asks Lynn.

"A yawn, a leak, and a good look round."

Sharon laughs and then quizzes them both. "What is it with you Aussies and your drinking? I was on a cruise once with my parents, and we spent some time with the Australians aboard. My God, they could drink!"

"Of course," says Dennis. "We know how to enjoy life. But you never saw any of 'em stonkered did you?"

"Stonkered?" asks Sharon, amused.

George and Dennis laugh and look at one another. George is the first to speak. "I guess we do have a few words to describe someone who's stonkered—drunk."

Dennis continues. "Yeah—'skin full,' 'tanked,' 'legless,' 'blotto,' 'pissed,' 'gutst,' 'hammered,'—"

George interrupts to add to the list: " 'charged,' 'slaughtered,' 'rotten,' 'smashed,' 'off one's tits,'—"

"What! You're making this up," says Lynn.

"No, ma'am—and we're just getting started. But, you gotta understand, you'll never see any of our countrymen 'under the influence.' We may look like it, but we're just having fun. Hey, enough about us. Let's hear your story."

"That's fair," agrees Sharon. "We're a lot like you two in that we've been best friends since high school. Cal was after us, but we wanted a real education, so of course we chose Stanford. Lynn's an artist and a musician—no surprise, since her father's a conductor and her mom owns an art gallery in Carmel. She could be a professional in either any time she wants. But, she'd rather teach—go figure."

"So, this volleyball stuff ..."

Lynn quickly responds. "Hey, that's what's *really* important! We're thinking about hitting the pro beach circuit soon."

"And you?" George quizzes Sharon.

It's now Lynn's turn. "Seriously, here's a gal who should be a pro golfer right now. Club champ at her course—a scratch golfer, and she doesn't even work at it. She was the best student in our high school. Dean's list every semester at Stanford."

"What's your major, Sharon?" asks Dennis.

Lynn answers for her. "Undeclared, ever since she started. She can do anything she wants, but what that is she can't figure out. Gotta make up her mind one of these days."

"I can always be a teacher's aide for you," teases Sharon.

George stands and offers a hand to Sharon. "What about that moonlight walk you talked about?"

With her hand still holding his, they move to the water's edge and begin their walk down the beach. In the far distance the twin smokestacks of the Moss Landing Power Plant may be seen silhouetted against the skyline. Though their hearts and minds are racing, a failure to find the appropriate words to convey their feelings leads to an awkward silence that lasts for several minutes. Finally, George summons the courage to speak. "Sharon, I know I'm running the risk of sounding pretty stupid, but it's a risk I'll have to take. I'm feeling kind of panicked because my time here is so limited, and the thought of leaving before ... I know I'm saying too much—too soon ... God, you see what I mean? I'm like a babbling idiot. The truth is I was totally unprepared for what happened to me today. I know this sounds pretty damn ... 'corny,' is that the word?—but the moment I saw you I felt something I've never felt before. You're the most fascinating girl I've ever met. Jesus, see what I mean? I know you think I'm a cheeky bloke, but …"

Sharon stops and turns to look at him as she takes his other hand. "No, I don't."

"You don't?"

She slowly moves close to him and reaches up to give him a kiss.

The Flight Attendant places her hand on Sharon's shoulder and awaits a reaction. When she receives none, she lowers Sharon's tray. Instantly, Sharon's eyes open and seek a reason for the intrusion. "Sorry to disturb you, but we're about thirty minutes from Dallas. Thought you might like a cup of coffee."

XVIII

EVEN THOUGH IT IS VERY early morning, the heat is oppressive. A door in front of the United Airlines main counter slides open, and Sharon, carrying one small bag, exits the main terminal of the Dallas International Airport. She looks around, spots a line of taxis, and heads for them. Seeing her approach, the driver of the cab next in line steps forward to greet her.

"G'Day."

Sharon stops short and smiles. "Sounds mighty like a countryman to me."

"Proud Aussie, ma'am. Happy to be of service."

"I'd like to use you the whole day and most of the night. Any objections?"

"No, ma'am."

"Enough of that ma'am stuff. Name's Sharon. What's yours?"

"Stanley."

"Where you from, Stanley?"

"Born 'n raised in Perth."

"Best beaches in the world. Well, Stanley, I don't know my way around Dallas, and I've got a lot of places to go. And, I have a six o'clock flight in the morning. Okay?"

"Okay by me."

"How much?"

"How far we goin'?"

"Don't really know. What's say I trust you, and you trust me. This'll get you started." She hands him two hundred dollar bills. "Sound fair?"

"I'm your man."

Inside the cab, Stanley looks over his shoulder. "Where to, ma'am?"

"One more time, Stanley. Get rid of that ma'am stuff."

"All right—Sharon—where we goin'?"

"What do you know about DE?"

"What part you talkin' about? The schools? The plant? What?"

"Isn't this where they're made? The boxes—'HiDEM's."

"Sure is. You want to see the plant, then? We're not far away."

"Let's start there."

Stanley touches the screen and the taxi pulls away from the curb.

Sharon continues, "Be a tour guide. Tell me a little about Dallas as we go, and everything you know about DE."

Stanley thinks for several seconds before responding. "Well, Dallas has the biggest plant in the country. Where it all got started."

"Lot's 'a people work there?" asks Sharon.

"Jesus, I'll say."

"Know any of them?"

"Sure."

"They like their job?"

"Never heard anyone complain. Good pay, good working conditions, good benefits. I'd say they're pretty happy."

"Has it been here long?"

"Let's see … about fifteen years I guess. Keeps getting bigger every year."

"What do they make there?"

"Hell, everything, far as I know."

"What does 'everything' mean?"

"I dunno'. The 'boxes,' as you call them. And all the programs … the 'audi-vids,' or whatever they're called."

"Sounds like they might make a little money."

Stanley laughs. "I couldn't even guess how much."

As they move through the city, Stanley continues to point out what he feels might be places of interest as he was originally instructed. Sharon, staring blankly out the window, appears to be oblivious to Stanley's efforts. He soon becomes aware of her preoccupation and stops speaking.

"There it is." He points to a monstrously large building on his left. "Their whole operation covers something like a square mile. Wanna' go inside?"

"Can I?"

"Sure. They got tours all day long."

"Stanley, how would you like to be a mate and help me?"

"Help you do what?"

"I figure two sets of eyes and ears are better than one. Just having you with me would make it easier and make what I'm doing seem more legitimate."

"Are we planning a heist, or are we gonna' bump off a bloke?"

Sharon laughs and gives him her full attention. "You really are a ripper of a mate. You know, I'm hungry. What's say I treat you to a sanger and a middy before we go in? I'll have brekky, and tell you what's goin' on."

In a small restaurant, Stanley works on his sandwich and glass of beer while Sharon has breakfast.

"How long you been here in Dallas, Stanley?"

"Three years, give or take a few weeks."

"You did say Perth, right?"

"Born 'n raised."

"None of my business, but what made you leave?"

"I was kickin' around, working in construction mainly, and I met this lady from the States who was there on vacation. We got somethin' goin', and I followed her here."

"To Dallas?"

"No. She lived in Atlanta. It didn't work out, so I came to see an uncle who lived here, and I just stayed."

"How'd you get started driving taxis?"

"It's my uncle's business. He set me up in a cab … the money was pretty good, and well … here I am."

"Been back to Perth?"

"No, but I'm puttin' money aside each month and plan to go back as soon as I can. Don't know what I'll do there, but … hell, it's still home. You said you'd tell me what's goin' on with you. Do you mind?"

"No, but it's a doosie of a story. You may think I'm off my trolley."

An hour later, Sharon and Stanley have become part of the ten o'clock tour at the main DE assembly plant. They, along with about a hundred people, are treated to a spectacular demonstration of the *Wonders of Dormant Enhancement,* featuring a host of singers and dancers who one would think came straight from a floor show in Vegas. The glitz and glamour of the Broadway spectacular has given Sharon and Stanley the freedom to slip away and wander the halls of the administration building.

They enter an office labeled *Research,* and Sharon approaches a woman behind a desk who appears to be a receptionist. "Excuse me, may I speak to the Director?"

The woman looks up and offers a quizzical smile. "Mr. Mays is not in. Did you have an appointment?"

"No, but he said to drop by at my convenience."

"Mrs. Roget is in. Would you like to speak to her?"

"Yes, please."

"One moment. May I ask your name?'

"Denton. Mrs. Denton."

The secretary disappears into a room marked *Private*. A minute later she reappears followed by an officious-looking woman in her early fifties.

"Hello. My name is Elizabeth Roget. You wanted to speak to Mr. Mays?"

"I had hoped to. He told me to drop by anytime."

"He's not here today, but perhaps I can help."

"Thank you. My name is Kathy Denton, and this is my associate, Mark Tichenor. We're from the Australian Education Association. Mr. Mays said he might be able give us some information."

"He didn't say anything to me about that, but I'll do my best to provide the information you need."

"That's very nice of you. I'll only take a few minutes of your time."

"Let's go into my office."

Sharon and Stanley follow Mrs. Roget and are offered a seat. Sharon immediately quizzes her host. "Specifically, what's the scope of your research? That is, what kinds of things do you test, and what do you hope to develop for the future?"

Mrs. Roget laughs. "I'm afraid that would take me days to describe. We've published a book that serves as a report of our findings along with a description of the areas of future investigation. Would that help?"

"It certainly would. I assume you have several recent graduates working here. Would it be possible for me to ask them a few questions?"

"I think I can arrange that. Would four or five be an adequate number?"

"Perfect. Also, since we're in the process of adopting DE, I wonder if you could provide me with a list of the groups or organizations that currently offer opposition to the program?"

The furrow in Mrs. Roget's brow prompts an immediate explanation from Sharon. "You see, we're still in the philosophical stage. We're hoping to identify every argument the other side might make, so we can effectively counter their opposition."

"I see. After the splendid results of our program, there really isn't any opposition of note. The few groups who do oppose our work remain underground because their activities defy established law. A few have received the right of protest under the freedom of speech amendment. You can imagine the degree of influence their efforts receive here. I can jot down the names of a few groups or individuals you might wish to contact if you think it will be of any value."

"Thank you. When would you like me to speak to the graduates?"

"Would thirty minutes be okay?"

"Great. Give us a chance to look around a bit. Ready, Mark?"

As soon as Sharon and Stanley leave the office, Mrs. Roget walks to a control unit and pushes several buttons. Then she picks up her cell phone and punches in several numbers. The furrow in her brow reappears.

Sharon and Stanley sit in the D.E. cafeteria having a cup of coffee.

"Stanley, you said you know some people who work here, didn't you?"

"Yeah."

"Do you suppose you could find out where they work and get in touch with them today?"

"I dunno. They probably work different shifts."

"Would you try?"

"Sure."

"Tell 'em I'd just like to talk to them for a few minutes. Have 'em bring along any of their mates they'd like. I'll buy all the beer they can drink."

"All they can drink?"

"All they can drink! You try to get in touch with them while I talk to the graduates. Okay?"

"I'll do my best."

Five exceedingly bright looking and well-groomed young people, ranging in age from seventeen to twenty, sit around a table facing Sharon. After the brief introductions are made, the three girls and two boys pay close attention as Sharon finishes offering her reasons for talking to them. As she does so, Sharon notices the small camera in the corner of the ceiling.

Sharon begins her questioning. "First, may I assume your experiences with Dormant Enhancement were positive?" Each graduate smiles and nods his/her head.

"Any complaints or problems any of you have with the program?"

A vigorous shaking of the head by each makes clear their feelings.

Sharon continues. "Did any of you find it hard to be separated from your parents? One by one, please. Lani?"

"No."

"Angelina?"

"I'm not sure I understand. We really weren't separated."

"Could you explain?" asks Sharon.

"I saw my parents' images every day and heard their voices. We were as close as we could be."

"Shawntee?"

"I agree with Angelina."

"Anthony?"

"No problem."

"Clarice?"

"If anything, I'd say it brought us closer."

Sharon decides to pursue a different course. "Have any of you had any adjustment difficulties after graduation?"

The young people look at one another, smile, and shake their heads. Shawntee offers an explanation for their response. "I don't think we've ever had more fun than when we were in DE. It was hard to leave, but we're okay."

"Then there must be some kind of adjustment problem," adds Sharon.

"Not really," says Anthony. "Most of what we had is still available to us."

"You mean ... with the use of your H.D.E.M? Do you all have one?"

All nod.

"Are any of you in a college or university?" queries Sharon.

All raise a hand.

Fascinated, Sharon continues. "Majors set? Futures clear? Clarice, how about you? What are your plans?"

"I enter Texas Tech in the Fall. I plan to become a chemical engineer."

"And when did you decide this?"

"While I was in DE. It was what I was told I was best suited for by our leaders."

"Shouldn't that be your choice?" asks Sharon.

"Sure, but we all need lots of advice and help."

"From?"

"Parents and our leaders," explains Clarice.

Shawntee is quick to add, "We listen to our leaders. They're the ones with the experience."

Sharon pauses to absorb the meaning of what she's hearing. "Okay, to change the subject, have you chosen a political party?"

In unison, the group vigorously nods their heads just as the door opens and Mrs. Roget enters. She smiles apologetically at Sharon and announces, "I'm so sorry, but I've kept these youngsters away from their duties. I'm afraid they have to get back to work as soon as possible."

Without comment, they all rise and move toward the door. Each turns and smiles at Sharon as they move through the door. With only the two adults remaining, Mrs. Roget's tone changes. "Mrs. Denton, for our records I need some verification of your position and status with your association. May I see your identification?"

"I'm sorry, my associate has my briefcase. Our credentials and letters of introduction are in it. He'll be here shortly, and I'll give them to you immediately. Will you be in your office?"

Mrs. Roget is slow to accept Sharon's explanation but finally says, "All right, you may join me in my office until he gets here."

"Fine, but I need to be excused for a moment. I have to use the powder room. I'll be right back." Before Mrs. Roget is able to respond, Sharon tosses her a quick wave of her hand and exits. Mrs. Roget can only watch her leave.

Outside the DE plant Sharon and Stanley walk toward the cab.

"Did you have any success with your mates?" asks Sharon.

"Talked to five of 'em, and they thought it was a bonzer of a plan! Said they'd stay long enough for you to write a book if you keep the grog comin'."

"What time do they get off?"

"Five. Told 'em where we'd meet."

"Great. Good timing."

Back in the cab, Sharon consults her notes. "What do you know about the *Dallas Daily News*?"

"Read it every day. Wanna see my copy?"

"I have an appointment at their offices. Know where that is?

"Sure."

"That's our next stop."

Sharon is ushered into a cluttered office by a young intern. He excuses himself to the person behind the desk and announces, "This is Mr. Fields." The intern immediately exits, closing the door marked *Managing Editor* behind him, leaving Sharon to face the man behind the desk. Richard Fields rises, walks around his desk, and extends his hand.

"Ms. Bradbury, nice to meet you in person."

"Please call me Sharon. Thank you for your time."

"Happy to help." The editor points to a chair, inviting Sharon to sit. "Nice flight?"

"It was fine."

"Ever been to Dallas?"

"My first time."

"Several things you might want to see while you're here—"

"I'm afraid I don't have time for much sightseeing. I have to leave tomorrow."

"Oh. Well then you'll want to get right down to business. I'll call Lorraine."

Sharon sits at a table in the pressroom having a cup of coffee. The editor and a woman in her early forties enter and walk to where Sharon is seated. Mr. Fields smiles and places his hand on the reporter's shoulder. "This is Lorraine Pruitt, Ms. Bradbury."

Sharon stands and extends her hand. "Very kind of you to talk to me, Lorraine. My name is Sharon."

Satisfied he's completed his task, Mr. Fields steps back and addresses Sharon. "Well, I've got some business to take care of. Let me know if I can be of any further help."

The two watch him leave and take a seat. Sharon is the first to speak. "Thanks for your time. I just have a few questions."

"Shoot."

"What, exactly, is the nature of your assignment? That is, are you looking for anything specific?"

"Not really. There's interest in DE all over the country but particularly so here in Dallas. The paper feels a certain responsibility to the readers to keep them informed. The series will be a kind of historical perspective. You know, showing what it's accomplished since it started."

"Then it's not the result of any recent … complaints?" asks Sharon.

"On the contrary. Almost everyone is extremely proud of the program."

"You say 'almost everyone.' Are there any detractors?"

"Well, there's always going to be a few who see problems in anything," explains Lorraine.

"Such as?"

"There are groups spread around the country who still fight to keep their children out of the program. Their numbers were much larger in the beginning, but after seeing what it's been able to accomplish, those numbers have dwindled significantly."

"Sounds like you think the program is …"

Lorraine waits for Sharon to finish her thought. Finally: "Successful? Yeah, I'd say so."

"Anyone complain about the cost?"

"The cost? No. Essentially, the cost is born by the taxpayer. And it's certainly a lot less expensive than it was in the dark days."

"The dark days? You mean ... before DE?"

"Maybe that's a little harsh. I think the schools were doing the best they could, but they were getting progressively worse. They just couldn't deal with society's problems."

"Society's problems? What about the kids?"

"Okay. Same thing," admits Lorraine.

"You say the cost today is a lot less than before DE. How can that be?"

"Well, it certainly is if you consider the results. I can check my notes if you'd like the exact figures, but roughly the average expense per student in the public schools was over $9,000 per year. For twelve years of a child's public school education the cost amounted to over $100,000. You might say it was worth it, but almost everyone admitted that students were not receiving a true quality education. The national high school graduation rate was barely over 70%. And our ranking in student achievement when compared to other countries was continuing to plummet."

Sharon interrupts, "But the cost of DE must be enormous."

"Oh, it was costly at first, through the research and development stage that is, but since it's become established the costs have continued to decline remarkably. Don't forget, the major reduction in the number of teachers and administrators, their union benefits, enhanced utilization of educational facilities, transportation costs—and on and on—have led to extremely significant reductions in costs. But, the most important consideration of all is the meteoric climb in graduation rates. Failure to graduate is enormously costly to a society in more ways than can be measured monetarily. Education pays, and interrupting it can be very expensive."

"The cost I was referring to is for the purchase of the HiDEMs—am I using the correct term?"

"Yeah, that's what most people call them. But are you talking about what the schools use, or what's available to the general public?"

"They're not the same?" asks Sharon.

"Well, they're similar."

"Okay, what about the cost of the ones people buy?"

"Actually, they're relatively inexpensive," explains Lorraine. "The cost has been coming down each year. And they're doing some amazing things."

Frustrated with the way the discussion is going, Sharon changes the subject. "The reporter who disappeared ... what were his notes like?"

"To be honest, I haven't seen them. I couldn't find anything here he'd written, and we've pretty much avoided talking to his wife out of respect for her situation."

"So now you're working with the people at DE? Are they cooperative?"

"It's almost embarrassing. They treat me like a celebrity. Well ... the PR people at least. They've given me several personal tours, opened their books to show how successful—and honest—they are. Given me everything I asked for. The R & D people aren't quite so open. They're probably afraid I'll steal some of their secrets. You know, run to a competitor who wants to jump on their money train."

"You've been very helpful. One last question. What's the name of the reporter who disappeared?"

"Rudy Melone," answers Lorraine.

"And his wife's name?"

"Melanie. But I hope you don't intend to talk to her. She's got enough on her mind right now."

"Of course not!"

Sharon stands on the front steps of a two-story Colonial in a nice neighborhood. The door opens and a woman dressed in a basic navy blue warm up suit stands in the opening.

"Yes?"

"Mrs. Melone? I'm very sorry to bother you. We've not met. I'm Marsha Kinsella from the *News*. We're trying to continue the series on DE your husband was working on. I apologize for the imposition, but I wonder if it would be too much trouble to see Rudy's notes?"

"I'm afraid I know almost nothing about what he's done on that assignment. The police took his computer and other records they thought might be helpful. I haven't heard a thing from them for some time now."

"I understand. Well … we thought it'd be worth checking. Again, please forgive me for this interruption. Thanks for your time."

Sharon turns and walks toward the waiting taxi. She stops as Mrs. Melone calls out to her. "Miss Kinsella?" Sharon takes several steps back in her direction. "I did find a folder in Rudy's dresser the other day. It looks like something he was working on at the paper. I didn't think to mention it to anyone, and I couldn't make much sense out of it, but it might have something to do with DE. You're welcome to look at it if you'd like."

Stanley holds the door open for Sharon who is busy shuffling through the contents of a manila folder. He takes his position behind the wheel and remains quiet as he waits for further instructions. Finally, "What's next?"

Lennie's Bar, a particular favorite of the DE workers after their shift on weekends, is unusually crowded and raucous. In the center of the room a dozen schooners of beer rest on a large table that is surrounded by at least the same number of workers from the plant. The waitress sets down two new pitchers and takes some money from Sharon. Though she clearly enjoys the camaraderie with her new friends, Sharon's pleasure does not interfere with her ability to glean the information she is seeking. Across the bar, two men watch and listen as best they're able.

.

Hours later, while Stanley sits alone at a small table near the entrance, Sharon talks with a solitary young man in a secluded corner of a dimly lit dive. Nervous, the man with Sharon looks around often to make sure they're not being watched. Finally, Sharon slips the man an envelope, and he quickly stands and exits.

XIX

THE MONTEREY COUNTY COURTHOUSE, A mix of 1930 and 1960 era buildings, located in Salinas, stands in stark contrast to the nearby modern National Steinbeck Center. Sharon, weary and disheveled, rushes through the door of the courthouse, looks around, sees Patrick and Dennis sitting on a bench in the hall in deep conversation. Both see her at the same time and quickly rise.

Dennis gives her a kiss on the cheek and Patrick gives her a quick hug. "We'd just about given up on you."

Sharon is upbeat and excited, though the dark circles under her eyes clearly reveal a need for sleep. Her frenetic desire to convey her information results in an almost incoherent babbling. "God, guys, it was amazing! I hated to leave! I'm—I was—"

Patrick takes her hand in his, offers a smile that conveys the patience of an approving father, and very gently says, "Take a breath, sweetheart."

Sharon quickly calms, returns the smile, and continues, this time fully under control. "The information you wanted came pretty easily. But that's not the good stuff. I tell you there's something awfully dirty going on back there."

"Like what?"

She reaches in her purse and produces a packet with a rubber band wrapped around it. "I really don't know. It's not any one thing all by itself. It's a combination of a whole bunch of things. Okay, sounds crazy I know, but there's so much here that I haven't had time to put it all together. I've got a list of names a foot long. Most of them come from a reporter doing a story on DE who's now missing."

"Missing?" says Dennis.

"Yeah. That's kinda strange, don't you think? He started to dig up some stuff on DE and then he disappears?"

"Let's not make too much of this," cautions Patrick. "What did the police say?"

"Not much, but they don't know the whole story."

"And neither do you."

Sharon continues. "I'm only here because I have to be. I'm going back as soon as I can."

"You're due in court, young lady," explains Patrick.

"I tell you, this is our case!" insists Sharon. "We can't let this chance get away from us."

Patrick looks at Dennis. "Could you—"

"Yeah, sure. I'll look through it. I wouldn't be able to do much in there anyway." He takes the packet from Sharon. "Where do I start with all this?"

"I tried to make some notes on the plane trip back. I'll have to explain some of the stuff, but I think you can see where I'm headed."

"Okay." Dennis gives Sharon a long, hard look. "You're sure that all this isn't just wishful thinking?"

"Positive!"

Inside the courtroom, Judge Lungren bangs his gavel, and everyone, except Patrick and Donald Bartleby, the District Attorney, takes a seat.

Judge Lungren speaks, "The record shall disclose that all members of the jury are present. Counsels, are you ready to proceed?"

"Yes, Your Honor," says Bartleby.

"Ready, Your Honor," responds Patrick.

"You may begin, Mr. Bartleby."

Bartleby remains standing as Patrick takes his seat. "Thank you, Your Honor." He faces the jury as he speaks. "Ladies and gentlemen of the jury. I'm sorry that you're being forced to waste your time adjudicating an issue that should have been laid to rest long ago ..."

Later that morning, Bartleby continues to speak to the jury: "... we will show that the defendant in this case, Sharon Bradbury, willfully defied this statute by withholding her son, Eric, from the public school in his district of residence. The law is quite clear in this instance, and Mrs. Bradbury's intent to violate the law is a matter of record. But, ladies and gentlemen, the truth is that once again the system that has become the savior of this great society must be defended against those who would destroy it. Do not, for one moment, forget that it is Dormant Enhancement that is on trial here today."

Later still, Bartleby wraps up his remarks: "... My opponent will ask you to make one small exception to the law of our land in the name of 'personal freedom.' Let us not forget the painful lesson we learned in the past when freedom without responsibility led us to moral decay and to the brink of the destruction of our society." He takes his seat.

Judge Lungren looks at Patrick. "Mr. O'Connor, your opening statement."

Patrick stands. "Thank you, Your Honor." He walks to where the jury is seated and holds up a picture of Eric. "Take a good look at the morally decadent creature just described. This is the evil force you were told threatens to bring us to the brink of destruction … the insidious individual against whom we must marshal all our forces."

He hands the photo to one of the jurors. "Looks pretty innocent to me. Looks more like a young man who has been the best student in his class every year since he started school six years ago. In fact, he looks more like the perfect image of what our forefathers had in mind for their future. At twelve he is capable of doing every job required to run a 10,000-acre ranch in the Australian Outback. He's bright, responsible, fun, enthusiastic. Hardly the awful threat Mr. Bartleby described that threatens to bring our country to its knees …"

It is late afternoon, and the trial has ended for the day. Sharon and Kristen have stopped at a supermarket to pick up some groceries before returning home. Sharon, totally preoccupied with thoughts of the trial and walking like a zombie, pushes the cart as she follows her mother. In a deserted aisle, and with her mother some distance away, Sharon has come to a stop. A voice, several feet away, breaks her concentration.

"Mrs. Bradbury."

Sharon looks in the direction of the voice and sees a couple in their mid-forties examining a product on the shelf in front of them. They turn and move to the other side of the aisle as the woman continues to speak.

"Please don't look at us. It's best that we not be seen together. My name is Helen. This is my husband, Martin. Pretend to read a label or something." Though confused, Sharon does as she has been asked.

The woman continues. "We know about your problem with DE. We're with an underground group called *Free the Children*. Have you heard of us?"

"No. Well, maybe I have."

"It's a group of parents who refuse to have their children put in DE. We've been able to keep our kids with us, but we have to stay hidden, of course."

"Where?"

"I'm sorry, but I'm not at liberty to say."

"How many of you are there?"

"There are about fifty in our group, but there are groups like us all over the country. Please understand that we're taking quite a risk even talking to you, but we're here to offer you help."

"How?"

"There's lots we can do, but just knowing there are others like yourself may give you some comfort. I don't have time to explain. I'm leaving some information on top of the cans where I'm standing. Please pick it up after we leave, read it, and be sure to destroy it when you finish."

Kristen's voice, coming from the end of the aisle, interrupts them. The couple quickly walks away.

"What are you doing?" quizzes Kristen.

"Just reading labels."

That night, the three comrades sit around a table in the Bradbury den. Sharon's packet is open, and the contents are spread about. Patrick is reading the note from the parents Sharon encountered in the supermarket.

"It doesn't give you much to go on. A P.O. box, a phone number, a statement of their philosophy, and not much else. They said they could help?"

"That's what they said."

"How?" asks Dennis.

"There wasn't enough time for them to say."

"Well ... I think it's too risky right now," says Patrick. "We're in deep enough as it is. It's best that we concentrate on the problem we face in court. Maybe later if we run out of options, but right now ... Dennis, what have you come up with?"

"I don't know," says Dennis. "It suggests a lot, but there's no real evidence to back it up. For example, it's clear they have a monopoly on the production of almost everything relating to the program, but that's not unreasonable since their team of scientists were responsible for its development. They were careful to apply for the proper patents and, to a large extent, it's a non-profit operation, for the schools anyway. So ... what's to be gained?"

Sharon interrupts, "But ..."

"But what?" Dennis continues. "Where's the evil in that? I can't find any evidence that anyone's getting rich on it. I don't see anything in the reporter's notes to suggest anything like that. Schools cost money—and by the way, one hell-of-a-lot less than they used to."

"How could that be?" challenges Sharon, "Those ... machines gotta cost a lot of money."

"Well, sure." explains Dennis. "But so did teachers, and they had to be paid every year, even after retirement. And the sea of administrators—it was shown that New York City alone had more administrators than all the nations of Europe. Think how many it took throughout the country to run an educational system. Now, at least the way I understand it, the best minds in the country have created a standardized set of procedures and methods that can be carried out by a relatively small number of people. That's why the teacher's union fought it tooth and nail in the beginning. Clearly, most were about to lose their jobs. Of course some moved into administrative positions with the job of figuring out how to meet the individual needs of the students, but it was different and unfamiliar, and quite a few continued to fight it. But, over time, it became clear that even those who were responsible for the programming preferred it to the old system that required them to discipline and meet with parents. And many others chose to move to the lower grades, which made it less stressful."

Patrick finally weighs in. "Sounds like a good argument the way you express it, Dennis, but I think I agree with Sharon."

"In what way?"

"I think it's shitty!"

They all laugh. With the tension now broken, Sharon fills everyone's glass with some of Patrick's prize wine and raises her own. "To the demise of a shitty system!" Their glasses clink, and they each take a sip. Patrick's smile quickly disappears as he reminds the others, "Let's not forget we have to be in court tomorrow. Did you come up with anything that might help, Dennis?"

"Maybe. The reporter did run into a lot of opposition from the people who were responsible for the programming. Not with the curriculum exactly—more like the 'information' that was being transmitted to meet students' individual needs. There seemed to be some interference by ... some 'accusations' made by a few individuals about the qualifications of those in charge. He listed lots of names and suggested the need to follow a lot of leads. It's hard to describe, but he certainly had some suspicions."

"There you are!" adds a triumphant Sharon.

Patrick smiles and looks at Sharon. "The law requires a little more than a few vague suspicions." Sharon starts to speak but thinks better of it. Patrick continues, "But it is *something*." He looks at Dennis for several seconds before, "What do you think?"

Dennis takes an equally long time before he replies. "I'd say it's worth it. I know what you're asking. When do you want me to leave?"

Later that night, Sharon sits alone in the den nursing a glass of wine. A movie plays on a screen next to the simulated glow within the fireplace. Though she stares at the screen, her thoughts are clearly elsewhere. Finally, the debate within reaches its conclusion, and she downs the remaining wine before she pulls a folded piece of paper from her pocket. She re-reads the information carefully, then looks at the movie screen and says, "volume down." She turns in the direction of the painting and gives the command, "Screen." After the transformation occurs, she speaks to the blank screen, "Starfish – 8847." The screen remains blank for several seconds before the message "*Not Available— Leave a Message*" flashes on and off.

Sharon hesitates before she speaks, but when she does, it is with conviction: "Helen and Martin, this is Sharon Bradbury. Please let me know how I can talk to you. I need your help."

Located off Hecker Pass Highway, ten miles west of Gilroy, *Mt. Madonna County Park*, a majestic 3,700-acre recreational retreat, overlooks the Santa Clara Valley to the east. To the west lies Monterey Bay. Hikers and equestrians have access to a fourteen-mile trail system that winds through a pristine redwood forest. Nature lovers delight in the opportunity to walk for hours through the redwoods and oaks without seeing another soul.

As Sharon jogs along a trail in the park, she looks about often. Rounding a bend, she sees a woman seated at a picnic table in the deserted picnic site. The woman looks up, smiles, and offers a greeting as Sharon approaches.

"Hi, Sharon."

"Helen?"

"That's right. Any trouble with my directions?"

"No. This is a beautiful."

"And private," adds Helen. Sharon can't help but notice that Helen, though she appears to be about her same age, speaks in the manner of a woman much older. Is it the gravelly, smoker's voice—the unfashionable hairstyle?

Helen continues, "Sorry we didn't answer your call, but we do have to be careful. Obviously, you got the material I sent you, since you're here. Your message sounded a little desperate. Believe me, I know exactly where you're coming from. We experienced something similar only a few years ago."

"What happened?" asks Sharon.

"We left. That is, we took our daughter who was about to be forced to enter DE and went on vacation to Europe. We stayed as long as we could, but my husband's business… our families … were here. So we sneaked back, I guess you could say. We came into contact with a few others like ourselves and formed a little protective community where we could keep our kids. As you can imagine, we've had to keep all this secretive or we'd— well, I don't have to tell you what could happen."

"So ... how long—"

"Do we have to carry on like this? Our daughter will be sixteen this year, and then we hope we'll be done with all this. Of course we'll continue to give support to other groups like ours and to those who are trying to overturn DE in the courts."

"And you say you know of other groups like yours?"

"Yes. It's hard to know just how many, but they're there. And always ready to help."

"Help? What kind of help?" asks Sharon.

"Financial, for one. For another, security for the parents who've managed to keep their kids out of the program. Sorry to say we can't help you much in that area. Probably the major thing we have to offer is the moral support and understanding parents like you need. Just knowing you're not alone helps tremendously. Who's helping you now?"

"My parents. A close friend who was the best man in our wedding and an old law professor from Mendocino."

"Anyone else?"

"That's pretty much it," answers Sharon.

"How do they feel about your talking to us?" quizzes Helen.

"They don't know. They tried to discourage me after they heard about our contact at the grocery store."

"I can understand that. Maybe we should keep it that way. I can arrange a safe line of communication for the two of us. You never know just what you'll need. But please know this, we'll be there to help in any way we can."

Sharon is alone and about finished with the dinner dishes when her cell phone sounds. She picks it up, looks at the caller ID, and smiles.

"Hi, Lynn."

"Hi, hon. How you doin'?"

"Well, let's say I've seen better times. What about you?"

"I'm fine. Been thinking about you a lot. This shit you're going through is awful. Could you use a little break? I got some damn good wine that's gonna go bad if I don't use it up quick. Can you get away?"

"I think so. For a little while."

"Terrific! Wanna come here? It's quiet. Chance to catch up."

"Sounds heavenly. But I can't leave until I get Brock to bed. Okay?"

Two hours later at Lynn's beach house, a half empty bottle of Chardonnay sits on the table in front of the two friends. In the background Nora Jones' *"Sleepless Nights"* plays softly. Their attention is focused on a high school yearbook propped open in front of them.

Lynn laughs and points. "God, what the hell were we wearing?"

"I'd say we looked 'rad,'" concludes Sharon.

"What did we call that awful hair style?"

"Beats me. I don't think anyone could come up with a name to describe its ..."

"Ugliness?" offers Lynn.

"How did we see?" asks Sharon.

"Our poor parents. I remember my mother constantly brushing the hair out of my eyes."

Sharon agrees, "It's a miracle mine even tolerated me."

"Yeah," says Lynn, "I think I do remember a couple of confrontations."

"A couple! Per day you mean?"

Lynn laughs. Sharon continues, "I know I haven't been very understanding of their feelings with all the DE stuff."

"How so?"

"Well, if I'm really honest, I'd have to admit that I've made this whole business pretty much all about me. My parents loved George, too. And my mom now even admits, a bit reluctantly maybe, that she wasn't completely honest about this DE thing. Got us here cause she wanted to see her daughter—be with her grandkids. Not a lot different from what I've been obsessing about. What I'm saying is that I've not treated her fairly. And the tough part is, I haven't told her so."

"What did she say that got you here?"

Sharon continues, trying to find the right words. "She made it sound like we'd somehow be exempt from this ... required attendance thing. She led me to believe that dad had made some special arrangements. Truth is, I was too dumb to look into it and find out for myself. And I should have known. I even remember George and I talking about it when it first got started here. George thought it was pretty dumb, and I, believe it or not, thought it sounded like a good idea."

"Really?"

"Sure. Things were so screwed up here that I thought somebody had to do something. I knew it didn't affect us, so I really didn't find out as much as I should have."

"Okay, now that we're confessing our sins, I thought it made sense, too—at first. If nothing else, the lack of discipline on the part of young people seemed to justify any change in the way we did things."

"You said 'at first.' "

"Yeah," continues Lynn. "Pretty quickly I came to the conclusion that having a bunch of know-it-all zombies was even worse than having a few unruly shits."

When Lynn finishes speaking, they sit back to listen to the end of K.D. Lang's song, *"In Perfect Dreams."*

XX

AT ALMOST PRECISELY THE SAME moment that Dennis, carrying only one bag, steps off the curb in front of the Dallas airport and hails a cab, a man in his late fifties, William Lawrence, takes the witness stand in the Monterey Courtroom. Bartleby begins his questioning.

"Mr. Lawrence, for whom do you work?"

"The Federal Government."

"Department?"

"The Justice Department. I'm the Western Regional Deputy Commissioner."

"Then you're familiar with the compulsory education laws as they pertain to American citizens?"

"My office is responsible for their enforcement."

"How do you view Mrs. Bradbury's refusal to enroll her son in the Monterey Peninsula Academe Integral?"

"It's a clear violation of Section eighty-six of the Education Code."

Before Bartleby asks his next question, he looks at the jury and moves in their direction. "And what is the penalty for her violation?"

"Objection!" Patrick rises and addresses the judge. "Not only has this witness found my client guilty, but he's about to pronounce sentence."

"Sustained."

Bartleby walks back in the witness' direction. "Let me re-phrase. Do citizens of the United States have an obligation to follow the laws as set forth in the Education Code?"

"Certainly."

"And failure to follow those laws is a felony?"

"Absolutely."

Dennis and a man in his early fifties talk quietly at a table in the back of a seedy bar. The man is nervous, and he frequently looks over his shoulder.

104

Dennis reaches in his coat pocket, takes out an envelope, and sets it next to his drink before he rises and leaves. The man scans the room before snatching the envelope and shoving it in his pocket.

It is early afternoon. On the witness stand Dr. Martin Bauer, an expert on drug use and trafficking, is testifying.

"… from 1975 to 1995 we saw a slight decline in the use of Marijuana and hallucinogens, but a marked increase in the use of cocaine, heroin, and alcohol. By the early 21st Century two-thirds of the youth were regular drinkers. Two-fifths were frequent binge drinkers. It was obvious to most sociologists and psychologists that we were heading …"

Later that same day, boredom is written on the face of Sharon, and Patrick's level of frustration grows as the parade of witnesses continues.

Bartleby speaks to the current witness. "As a college president and an expert on public school education, would you describe some of the relevant trends in educational achievement before DE and after?"

"Objection!" Patrick slowly stands. "Again, DE is not on display here. We're concerned only with the rights of my client and her son."

Without bothering to look at Patrick, the judge calmly announces, "Overruled."

"Overruled? Have I wandered into the wrong courtroom? We're here to defend the rights of a citizen. They're intent on extolling the virtues of a system. Laws and courts are for people. Laws and—"

"Sit down, Mr. O'Connor! I'll not warn you again. Please continue, Dr. Sarnoff."

Dr. Sarnoff continues, all the while watching Patrick, expecting an interruption. "Before DE, schools were becoming a nightmare. By 2006, an average of almost 250,000 students carried a weapon to school, and daily some 250 to 300 students were shot, stabbed, or beaten during the school day. At the time experiments with DE were begun, approximately twenty per cent of all seventeen year-olds were functionally illiterate. We witnessed a steady decline in SAT scores beginning in 1969 and continuing well into the 21st Century. Between 1975 and 2015, attendance in remedial mathematics and English courses in public four-year colleges more than tripled. One hundred per cent of all community colleges and eighty-four per cent of four-year colleges offered remediation. This gap in the students' education alone cost our country in the tens of billions of dollars. Low high school graduation rates have long been used to demonstrate the failure of America's educational system, but they also had a devastating effect on the graduation rates of postsecondary institutions. Statistically, the colleges performed worse than high schools. They were graduating only about half of the students who entered their doors, principally because they were not academically prepared at the outset. The DE students have completely reversed that trend. Illiteracy among that age group today is unheard of. The highest achievers in our college's history are products of DE."

Dennis talks to a man at the front desk in his hotel and hands him a rather large sealed packet and a folded wad of money. They shake hands.

An hour later, Dr. Thornberg has replaced Dr. Sarnoff on the witness stand. Boredom continues its residence on the faces of both Sharon and Patrick as Bartleby queries the witness.

"Your school was one of the first to open, am I correct?"

"That's correct. It was one of twenty-six that became fully operational in April of 2017."

"Dr. Thornberg, you are one of the founders of the Dormant Enhancement program, aren't you?"

"That's correct. I was part of the President's Council on Education that was established in 2008."

"And what were the objectives of that Council?"

Patrick rises and speaks to the judge. "Your Honor, can we do without the history lesson?"

The judge speaks to the opposing counsel. "May we move along, Mr. Bartleby?"

"Your Honor, I'm merely trying to establish the reputation of both Dr. Thornberg and his school."

Patrick sighs deeply and looks at the jury. "For the record, we concede that Dr. Thornberg's been around a long time, and his school is … pretty."

Bartleby begins his objection, but the judge beats him to it. "Mr. O'Connor, I—"

"I'm sorry, Your Honor, but the reputation of Dr. Thornberg and his school is immaterial. As schools go, it's a good one, and Dr. Thornberg knows his business. Can we get on to something pertinent?"

Bartleby, becoming somewhat exasperated, moves to a position between the judge and Patrick. "Your Honor! May I be permitted to establish the facts in this case as I see fit? I'm sorry if my opponent is bored, but we're not here for his entertainment."

Patrick sits before the judge speaks. "You may proceed, Mr. Bartleby."

"Thank you. Once again, Dr. Thornberg, what were the objectives of the Council?"

"It was clear to everyone that the American educational system was failing. The Council's goal was simply to identify the reasons for this and to recommend changes."

"You're saying that the individual schools were not capable of accomplishing this on their own?"

"That's what I'm saying."

"Why?"

"There were many reasons. For one, each school district and each teacher was autonomous—that is, they were free to pursue their own methods and procedures—within certain limitations, of course. Some succeeded, but many failed. Individual teachers were free to practice what was commonly known as 'academic freedom.' "

"And that was?"

"To put it rather crudely, teaching was considered by many to be an 'art' rather than a science."

"And what's wrong with that?" asks Bartleby.

Thornberg continues. "On the surface, nothing. But it depends on the individual. Literally thousands of experiments were taking place in the classroom. Teachers were free to use any method they chose to accomplish their goals. As I said earlier, some succeeded, but many failed."

"This ... failure you speak of, is due to the incompetence of the teacher, then?"

"Oh, absolutely not. The growing pressures from society and from parents themselves made the teacher's job extremely difficult."

"What were these growing pressures?" inquires Bartleby.

"Objection!" Patrick stands. "Once again, Your Honor, all of this is immaterial to the case before us. Why are we—"

Judge Lungren stops him before he can finish. "Sit down, Mr. O'Connor."

Bartleby returns to a focus on the witness. "Please proceed, Dr. Thornberg."

"Well, let's look at the parents' interference. Though they might not admit it, every parent who places a child in the care of someone else hopes—in fact, expects—that the person will reinforce their values ... their beliefs. To put it a little differently, I think each parent would be thrilled to see their child become a 'clone' of themselves. And, it's not an illogical way to think. Why should their child *not* share their beliefs—have them further established and supported by the schools? And what do they often find? Just the opposite. The child ends up challenging their values and their views, and quite often a degree of hostility between parent and child is the result. It's passed off simply as a 'generation gap,' but the real truth is that it can become a wedge between them that often accounts for a lifetime of alienation."

"And DE was able to correct this?" asks Bartleby.

"Yes. Now each parent is consulted and involved in every aspect of the child's development," explains Thornberg.

"Earlier you mentioned the growing pressures from society," continues Bartleby. "Could you explain what you meant by that?"

"In an attempt to answer that, perhaps I should pose a question for every person here. 'How could a child during his formative years be expected to withstand the temptations of the day that are constantly placed before him?' The easy availability of drugs and their growing appeal. The media's concentration on lurid sex and violence. The proliferation of games as an escape from their academic responsibility. The countless numbers of bizarre expressions of 'individuality.' And on, and on. Very few parents had the time or the ability to provide proper supervision. And none of this takes into account the unbelievable number of hours of wasted time. Getting up in the morning, getting dressed, having breakfast, traveling to school, going from class to class, trying to either be patient in the learning process and wait for others to catch up, or trying to catch up themselves when the pace was too rapid for them. It was shown that there were no more than a few minutes a day a child was free from the thousands of interruptions that were shown to occupy the young mind. And who was held responsible when grades declined as the problems increased? Unfortunately and unfairly, it was the teachers and the schools. So, the conclusion was reached that if we were to make the necessary improvements, it had to begin there. As everyone knows, years of investigation and experimentation under the supervision of our best minds led us to our present system. I'm sure the experts you've scheduled have attested to the high degree of its success."

Patrick, unable to contain himself and loud enough for all to hear, grumbles a response, "They have, ad naseum."

Judge Lungren casts a severe look in his direction. "Be careful, Mr. O'Connor."

The lunch break has ended, and the trial has resumed. It is mid-afternoon. Dr. Thornberg finishes his testimony directed by Bartleby.

"... proud of every aspect of the operation. Our system is the best in the world."

"Thank you, sir." Bartleby returns to his seat and speaks to Patrick. "Your witness."

Patrick remains in his seat as he asks his first question. "Tell me, Dr. Thornberg, are you a graduate of the DE program?"

Thornberg smiles and looks at the judge. "Of course not. The first public DE school opened only a little over seven years ago."

"Well, did you go to school before that?"

Bartleby stands. "Your Honor, if Mr. O'Connor has a serious and legitimate question, let him ask it."

The judge looks at Patrick. "Mr. O'Connor?"

"Oh, but I'm quite serious. You appear to be an intelligent, well-educated man, Dr. Thornberg. I would say you're doing quite well in spite of the old-fashioned education that you and many of the rest of us in this courtroom received. Yet, you make this new-fangled approach to learning seem almost sacred."

Again Bartleby is on his feet. "Can we find a question somewhere in all this, Your Honor?"

Patrick smiles and bows to his opponent. "Dr. Thornberg, if the former method of education was good enough for you, and for all of us, then why would it not be adequate for my client's son?"

"Times have changed, Mr. O'Connor. And with it, the need for a new system. Our society was headed toward destruction, and DE has changed all that."

"Without DE, my client's son is an honor student. No drugs. No crime. No rebellion. Why has he been thrown into isolation?"

"Objection!"

"Withdrawn. Dr. Thornberg, you say that the schools were not capable of handling the problems on their own. Is that correct?"

"Yes."

"I hate to beat a dead horse, but you, and even I, seem to have turned out all right. Would you agree?"

"All right, Mr. O'Connor, I agree, but the times were different and the pressures were not so great."

"Really! Well, I don't know about you, but my parents thought I was going to hell in a hand basket because I listened to rock 'n roll. Ever watch Elvis shake his hips, Doctor? Of course you did. Ever read a novel under the covers with a flashlight? Sure you did. Ever have a few beers with the guys? Smoke a little pot?"

"Objection, Your Honor! Mr. O'Connor is both asking and answering his own questions."

"Mr. O'Connor!"

"I'm sorry, Judge, but I was afraid his answers might embarrass him. It would be awful for him to admit that he did all those terrible things. It must have been because he was under a lot of pressure because of a lack of proper supervision."

Bartleby continues his objection. "Mr. O'Connor, what does any of this have to do with the matter before us? Let him stick to the issue, Your Honor."

"Well now, when I stated that exact objection I was threatened with contempt. I'm waiting, Your Honor."

"Mr. O'Connor, there is a limit to my patience. If you continue to make a mockery of this trial, I *will* charge you with contempt."

"But I do consider these questions to be totally relevant. May I proceed?"

"Yes, but you've been warned."

"Thank you. Now, Dr. Thornberg, did you make your own choice when it came to the university you attended?"

"Yes."

"Were your parents gone? Not interested? What?"

"I listened to their advice."

"Oh, good. But *you* made the decision. Tell me, do you like baseball?"

"I don't know what that has to do with anything, but yes."

"Giants' fan? "

"No. The Dodgers."

"Them bums? Your parents must have been big Dodger fans as well."

"No. They were Yankee fans."

"Yankee fans? They're not even in the same league! How did your parents handle you being a Dodger fan?"

Bartleby starts to rise.

"All right, before anyone gets too excited about where I'm going with all this, let me beat him to the punch. You said something to the effect that parents would like the schools to give them back a 'clone' of themselves when they were finished. Is the freedom to *choose* so awful in our co-called 'free society?' And this business of dealing with pressure—some of us here remember a little of Viet Nam, the collapse of our economic system, most of us remember something about that Middle East debacle, and I'm sure we all know what it's like to fear another terrorist attack. In my way of looking at it, we faced a little pressure of our own as we grew up, and it hasn't exactly destroyed *us*."

Bartleby is on his feet again. "Your Honor, I wasn't aware that we had arrived at the point when we were to make our summation. The witness is on the stand for a reason. If Mr. O'Connor has questions for him, let him ask them. Otherwise, may the witness be excused?"

Patrick smiles at his opponent and continues. "All right, Dr Thornberg, let me ask you this. During your extremely interesting description of the history of American education, you described the reasons for the establishment of our system of compulsory education."

Thornberg quickly jumps on Patrick's statement. "I'm glad you were listening, Mr. O'Connor. It was found to be a human right based on Article Twenty-six in the 1948 Universal Declaration of Human Rights. Before compulsory free education, most children were denied access to a basic education. After it was established, illiteracy was reduced, and children became better prepared for their future professions and for better paying vocations. A major milestone, don't you think?"

Patrick, having remained patient until Dr. Thornberg had finished, addresses the judge. "Your Honor, would I be out of line to ask you to inform the witness that I'm the one who asks the questions?"

Judge Lungren speaks directly to Patrick. "Then move along and ask your question."

"I'm trying, Your Honor. Dr. Thornberg, is it possible that all schools, yours in particular, might be guilty of inhibiting the individual's ability to self learn? That they might be guilty of taking up a great deal of the child's free time as they impose their own standards and goals?"

Thornberg starts to answer, but Patrick raises his voice as he continues. "Guilty of denying individual liberty?"

Thornberg answers quickly, his voice rising. "Would you have us withhold access to a basic education for our citizens?"

"There he goes again, Your Honor."

"Dr. Thornberg, would you please limit your answers to Mr. O'Connor's questions."

"I'm sorry. What was the question?"

"As things now stand, Dr. Thornberg, parents are required to send their children to DE because they're incapable of providing the necessary cognitive skills and moral training. Is that correct?"

"It's not necessarily because they are incapable. All the evidence indicates that these objectives were not being met."

Patrick moves to a position next to the jury box. "How do we know? If all the young people are rounded up and herded into forced enclosures, what role is left for the parents to play?"

"Do you deny the results, Mr. O'Connor?" asks Thornberg.

"What results are you talking about?"

"I assumed you'd paid attention to the testimony of our experts these past three days."

"Oh, those results. I thought you might be referring to the results of those who chose home schooling—oh, forgive me, I forgot—we don't have that anymore. In our infinite wisdom we decided to deny our citizens the freedom to decide what was best for their children."

Thornberg quickly responds, addressing his comments to the jury. "As we all know, the matter was brought before the Supreme Court, and it was decided that for the better good of the whole, a few individuals might have to conform to practices that benefited all of us."

"In other words, they made home schooling illegal. And you said a *few* individuals. Do we know just how many that might be?"

Thornberg again addresses Patrick directly. "I have no idea."

"Really? I was sure an expert on educational matters would have some notion as to the number of Americans who found this approach to be repugnant."

"Repugnant? Look at the results!"

"I think we were talking about the numbers of people who suddenly became 'criminals' in the eyes of the law because they exercised their right to decide what was best for their child. Estimates run as high as several thousand Americans who were either imprisoned or forced underground."

"Preposterous."

Patrick smiles and raises both hands. "At last, we agree!" He moves toward Thornberg but stops when he sees a look of confusion on his face. "Oh, you meant preposterous as to the number of people? I thought you'd found the proper word to describe the loss of one more of our freedoms."

"Objection!" Bartleby stands.

Patrick continues. "Withdrawn. Dr. Thornberg, let's change course a bit. I wonder if you'd mind indulging me for a moment. I'm an 'old school' kind of guy, so I'm a little fuzzy on just how this new-fangled school works. Would you mind clearing up a few things?"

Thornberg's look reveals his lack of patience. "If I can."

"Thank you. Now, let's see, on the child's twelfth birthday he or she is required to enter DE?"

"Actually, it's the day after his twelfth birthday," adds Thornberg.

"Oh, okay. And the child must remain there until his sixteenth birthday when he graduates. Is that what you call it? Graduates?"

"That's what we call it. But let me correct you on one point. The student is not required to remain there for the full time without a break. They have a week at Christmas, a week in the summer, and the parents may chose three other occasions each year when the student may join them."

"For how long?"

"Two days."

"Two days. Let's see, two weeks ... and six days. That's twenty days away from DE. Isn't that kind of dangerous?"

Thornberg looks puzzled. "Dangerous?"

"Well what if the child likes it on the outside when he's on parole?"

"Objection!" interrupts Bartleby.

"Sustained. Be careful, Mr. O'Connor."

"Oh, gosh, I'm sorry. I didn't mean to offend. Dr. Thornberg, I ran across an editorial that appeared in the *New York Times* that suggested that the DE gurus were actually opposed to these 'vacations.' That they came about as a result of, let's see, (reading) 'pressure from the business community because they saw their sales slumping, and because the parents wanted to show off their kids.' Any comment, Dr. Thornberg?"

"No comment."

"May we then conclude that you agree with the opinion?"

"No, you may not!"

"So, you don't agree? Tell me, Dr. Thornberg, were you in favor of these 'vacations'?"

Thornberg hesitates before he responds. "To be truthful, I was not."

"Would you tell us why?"

Again, Thornberg hesitates. "It was an interruption of their educational progress."

Patrick scratches his head and looks at the jury. "An interruption of their educational progress? Is that another way of saying it screwed up your brainwashing?"

Judge Lungren interrupts. "Mr. O'Connor, we've had about all we can stand of your mockery. I hold you in contempt of this court and fine you $1000. I gave you repeated warnings. If you defy me again I will remove you from the courtroom and you will serve some time in jail. I trust I've made myself clear. We stand adjourned until ten tomorrow morning."

It is early morning of the next day. The sun is just beginning to make its appearance in downtown Dallas. Dennis leaves his hotel and hails a cab. After he enters and the taxi pulls away, a car, parked several spaces behind and containing two men, eases into traffic to follow.

Shortly after this, two men systematically tear apart Dennis' hotel room. They turn the mattress and chairs upside down, rummage through the drawers, and rip apart his clothing and suitcase. "Shit, this is a fuckin' waste of time. There's nothin' here."

On the other side of the city, nine well-dressed men are seated at a huge oak table in the dining room of the mansion in Dallas. Every eye in the room is riveted on the man standing before them as he speaks. Though now formally dressed, he is clearly recognizable as "the man in overalls."

"Now that you know the situation and what has to be done, I trust there will be no more fuck-ups!"

XXI

IT IS COOL AND FOGGY, a typical evening in Carmel. The curtains in the Webber den are open, but it is difficult to see beyond the head of the driveway. The simulated glowing fire provides a comforting contrast to the feeling of isolation the enveloping fog has created. Sharon and Patrick's concentration on separate legal briefs is interrupted by musical notes from the *1812 Overture* signaling an incoming call. Sharon turns toward a painting on the wall and says, "Screen." The painting is transformed into a TV screen on which appears a nice looking woman in her early forties.

"Mrs. Bradbury?"

"Yes?"

"I'm Catherine Gates, Brock's teacher."

"Oh, yes. Hi."

"Sorry to call you at night like this, but I've tried during the day, and your mother said you were busy."

"Yes, I have been busy. Is there a problem with Brock?"

"Well … yes, there is. All new students have a difficult time adjusting to a new situation, I know, but …"

"What's the problem?" asks Sharon.

"He's been in a couple of fights. And when we tried to talk to him about it, he was … frankly, quite hostile."

"Hostile?"

"He called us names. Used some rather abusive language."

"Like what?"

"Told us to 'bugger off,' or something to that effect."

"Oh, my, I'm sorry."

"The worst part is that he doesn't do his work."

"That doesn't sound at all like him. He's always been very interested in school."

"I'm sure that's true. I just wanted to call it to your attention. Maybe you can talk to him about it."

"I certainly will. And I'm terribly sorry that …"

115

"I know. He's clearly a bright boy. Something must be bothering him to make him act this way."

"I think I know what it is. I'm sure we can work it out. Thank you for calling."

Mrs. Gates' image disappears. Sharon stands and walks to the window. "God! What next?"

Patrick, who has been watching and listening, weighs in. "Sounds like he's acting out his fears. And missing Eric, I'm sure."

"That's exactly what he's doing."

Again the musical notes sound. Sharon moves to the center of the room and looks at the painting. "Christ, what now! Screen."

This time Dennis' image appears. He is tired. Nervous. "Sorry, guys. Did you think I'd jumped ship?"

"Where are you?" asks Patrick.

"Still in Dallas."

Patrick continues. "You found something?"

A sound in his room causes Dennis to jerk around. He disappears from the screen for a few seconds. When he returns, he is apparently convinced that it was nothing but his imagination. His paranoia has been replaced by an excited sense of conviction. "Jesus, have I! I just sent an ILOG. It should be there in a few minutes. At least I hope so."

"What do you have?"

"It's all in the ILOG. It's hard for me to keep it straight right now. I haven't had more than a couple hours of sleep since I left. I'll be there tomorrow morning. I can fill in the gaps then. But listen ... be careful!"

Patrick frowns, "Be careful?"

Sharon adds, "Of what?"

"I ... I just ... may have gone too far. Just be careful!"

Patrick walks to the screen and stands directly in front of it. "Dennis, what kind of trouble are you in?"

"I'm okay."

"You sure don't sound okay. Are you in danger? Call the police. Right now!"

"I don't have time. I'm meeting someone."

"Young man, you do what I say! I want you—" Dennis' image suddenly disappears. Patrick looks at Sharon with a look that says, "fix it."

Helpless, she can only stare at the reformation of the painting. Her command of "Screen," repeated several times, has no effect.

The sound of twelve tiny bells from an ancient mariner's clock, sitting next to several antique collectables on the bookcase, serves to heighten the pair's anxiety.

Patrick, doing his best to convey a lack of concern, stands, stretches, and announces, "Well, I'm going to bed."

"But … we can't until we get Dennis' ILOG."

"Obviously something's happened to it. And since we don't know how to get in touch with him, we'll just have to wait until tomorrow."

"You go ahead."

"You've done all you can, Sharon. We're just not going to hear from him tonight."

"I'm just not sleepy."

He walks to her, gives her a gentle pat on the head, and quietly leaves the room. Sharon remains immobile for a long time before she sits up, stands, walks to the window, and stares out at the fog.

Minutes later the door to Brock's bedroom quietly opens. Sharon enters and moves to Brock's bedside. She watches him for several seconds, then leans down and gives him a kiss. Before she leaves, she stops at Eric's empty bed and places her hand on his pillow.

XXII

THE MARKED CONTRAST BETWEEN THE Academe during the day and in the middle of the night is surprising. Even though a full range of activities continues round the clock, it appears relatively deserted as Sharon walks through the front door at 1:00 in the morning. Perhaps it is due to the darkness outside, or the total absence of visitors, or the dimmed lights in the corridors, or even the limited presence of administrative personnel, but an eerie feeling sweeps over her the moment she enters the foyer. And it continues until she stands in front of room 306.

She peeks through the small glass below the room's number, then pushes the door open slowly and looks in the direction of Eric's cubicle. Gradually her attention turns to an activated screen above. Concentric circles are shown pulsating as a voice repeats, "Order is all important. Look to your leaders to show you the way."

Interested, she watches and listens to the repetitive message. Finally, she moves farther into the room and is able to see a technician seated at the control panel. When he sees her for the first time, he quickly hits a button on the control panel, and the picture and voice disappear. He rises and walks toward her.

"Hello. I didn't see you come in. Can I help you?"

"No, thanks. I couldn't sleep, and I just thought I'd drop by. It is all right, isn't it? I was told we could come by anytime."

"Oh … of course. It's just … a little unusual to have someone at this time."

"What's the lesson?"

"Gosh, I don't know. Let's see …" He refers to a master sheet at the control panel. "Geography."

"Geography? That didn't seem much like Geography."

The technician pushes a couple of buttons, and a map of Europe appears on the screen with an accompanying fast-paced lesson. Sharon's confusion gradually disappears, and she takes a seat in front of Eric.

She remains there for about ten minutes deep in thought. At last, she stands, nods goodbye in the direction of the technician, and exits.

Outside the room she looks around for anyone in sight. No one. Puzzled, she tries to open another classroom door. Locked. Then another. Locked. Frustrated, she continues her course down the hallway, arrives at the elevator, and pushes the button.

In a small all-night coffee shop on the wharf in Monterey, Sharon sits at the counter sipping a cup of coffee. Two men enter and sit in a booth in back, all the while watching her. After a few minutes she drops some money on the counter, rises, and exits. Through the window of the restaurant, the two men continue to watch her as she walks toward her car. As soon as she gets in, they stand and move toward the door.

The winding *Ocean View Boulevard* that parallels the coastline provides a particularly scenic route from Monterey to Carmel. Though now fog-shrouded and deserted, Sharon chooses it over the more direct Highway 1 out of a sense of habit and desire to drive manually.

She moves along the road slowly, with *Rachmaninoff's Piano Concerto* serving as a background to her troubled thoughts. Sharon glances at the rearview mirror and becomes aware of a car following dangerously close. Is that a Lexus? It's sure as hell riding my ass. She slows and pulls to the edge of the road on the ocean side. The Lexus also slows to match her pace. She gives it a moment, but it refuses to pass. Screw it! She presses hard on the accelerator.

Her car picks up speed. She pushes it to sixty, but the Lexus accelerates to keep pace. What's he up to?

A bend in the road forces Sharon to slow. The Lexus shoots around her on the left, pulling into the oncoming traffic lane. Is he insane? Why wait to pass till they were on a curve? I gave him ample time to pass earlier when it was safe.

The Lexus continues to pace her, staying just to her left. Sharon tries to get a look at the driver, but the ominous, black-tinted windows hides his identity. Suddenly, the Lexus swerves toward Sharon.

The impact makes her car shudder. She fights hard to keep it on the road. My God, that maniac wants to kill me! Her car slams into the guardrail and sends sparks flying.

Sharon pushes back, managing to get a few feet of separation from the Lexus. She uses those few feet to accelerate, hoping to put some distance between her and the Lexus. The Lexus hesitates for a moment, and then shoots after her.

The guardrail disappears. Nothing separates her car from a hundred foot drop. He means to kill me, and now he has his chance. Her heart pounds fiercely, the blood throbs in her ears, muffling the roar of her engine. Could she out run him? She's not sure.

The Lexus continues to close, and Sharon grudgingly concludes it outmatches her car. Desperate, she decides to switch tactics. She waits till it slips around her and pulls alongside. She watches it closely because she realizes that timing is everything. If she miss-times this move, she'd be dead for sure.

The Lexus swerves. Sharon slams on her brakes. The Lexus clips her front end, but without her car to provide resistance, it shoots past her and over the side of the cliff.

Her car spins in a circle. She turns her wheels in the direction of the skid, managing to bring it to a stop before it follows the Lexus over the side. She sits gripping the steering wheel, her knuckles completely white. She gulps down several breaths before the dam breaks and the tears flow down her cheeks. She sobs, ashamed that she can't control her emotions.

•

XXIII

PATRICK IS ON HIS FEET facing the judge in court. "I apologize for my ill-chosen remarks, Your Honor. I thank you for allowing me to continue our case. Also, I apologize for my client's absence. She was taken ill and will not be able to be in court today. I trust we may proceed without her."

"Any objections, Mr. Bartleby?"

"No, Your Honor."

"Then you may continue."

Patrick adds, "Your Honor, may I ask one other thing of my esteemed opponent? Would the prosecution be kind enough to reveal how many more history lessons we have in our future? I'm not sure just how much time I have left in this life."

Bartleby is quick to respond. "Your Honor, we're delighted to hear of Mr. O'Connor's interest. Today we will again address drugs, crime, and juvenile delinquency—"

Patrick interrupts, "Let me guess—tomorrow's subjects will be famine, pestilence, and war."

The judge, tired of the banter, speaks to both. "Gentlemen, may we proceed?"

"The prosecution calls ..."

During a break in the morning session, Patrick and Sharon sit on a bench outside the courthouse.

"Are you sure you're all right? You don't have to be here, you know."

"I'm okay, but it did scare the hell out of me."

"When did you finish with the police?"

"Couple of hours ago. My dad's still there."

"You must be exhausted. Do they have any idea what it was all about?"

"No. They don't even know who it was. The car at the bottom of the drop off was empty. They checked all the hospitals. It's amazing they weren't killed. They sure as hell were trying to kill me. I *am* sure of that."

"My God, Sharon. Now I'm worried about you *and* Dennis. Maybe you should go home and get some rest. I'll handle everything here."

"I'm worried about Dennis, too. Where is he?"

"He had a reservation for a 7:30 flight. We know that. But it wasn't used."

"He never checked out of his room," says Sharon. "I've tried a dozen times to get some information from the hotel. His cell doesn't respond. Something's happened."

"I don't like it either, but what can we do? Will your mother—"

"Yeah. She knows to call me as soon as she hears anything."

"All right, here's what we'll do. You go home, get some rest, and wait until you hear from Dennis. I can—"

A voice interrupts Patrick. "Pardon me, are you Sharon Bradbury?" The two look up and see a courthouse page.

"I'm Sharon." The page hands her a note and retreats. Sharon opens it, reads, and then grabs Patrick's arm. "Dennis is dead."

"What!"

Tears spring from Sharon's eyes. "An accident ... on the way to the airport."

"Jesus! When did it happen?"

"It doesn't say. Monica's on her way there. I should ..."

"Go. I'll get things postponed here and join you as quickly as I can."

"God, Patrick, it's my fault."

"Don't be crazy."

With a look of resolve on her face, Sharon stands. As she walks away, she shouts, "Damn them all!"

XXIV

THE LOBBY IN THE SHERATON Dallas Hotel is unusually quiet for this time of the evening. Sharon enters and walks directly to the front desk. The clerk, a young woman, offers a friendly smile. "May I help you?"

"My name is Sharon Bradbury. I'd like to see Monica Hardin."

Another clerk, older and more experienced, sitting in front of a computer a few feet away, stops his work and looks at Sharon. "I'll handle this, Rachel." He rises and moves to replace his colleague in front of Sharon. "If you'll wait just a moment, please." He goes to the office behind the front desk and knocks on the door. It opens, and the clerk mutters a few inaudible words. Seconds later, a distinguished man in his early sixties steps out of the room and approaches the front desk.

"Mrs. Bradbury, my name is Phillip Knight. I'm the manager. Mrs. Hardin is in my office with the police. Would you come with me, please?" Sharon walks around the counter and follows the manager into his office.

Inside, Monica, seated and cried out, sees Sharon. She immediately rises and moves to give her a hug. A man, leaning on the manager's desk a few feet away, gives them time to speak to each other before he addresses Sharon. "Mrs. Bradbury, I'm Detective Cali. I spoke to your father earlier, and he's filled me in on your situation."

Monica, becoming emotional again, blurts out the information, "Someone broke into Dennis' room."

"What! You mean ... before he ..."

Detective Cali explains, "His things were still there."

"But I thought he was on the way to the airport," says a confused Sharon.

The detective continues, "So did we, at first. But he hadn't checked out."

"I spoke to him last night. He was supposed to arrive in Monterey this morning. We were going to pick him up."

"We confirmed that with the airlines. May I ask what your relationship to Mr. Hardin was?"

"He was the best man in my wedding. This automobile accident ... was he driving?"

"Yes, but there were no witnesses."

"Our understanding was that he had a 7:30 flight," adds Sharon.

"The accident took place at 3:30. Obviously too early for a 7:30 flight." Detective Cali continues, "You say 'our.' Who else was aware of this?"

"Patrick O'Connor—and my parents. Dennis and Patrick were working together on a case in court."

"What was the nature of Mr. Hardin's business in Dallas, Mrs. Bradbury?"

"He was following some leads in our court case."

"May I ask the nature of your case?"

"It's a ... custody matter."

"Are you aware of the details of his business here in Dallas?"

"When he called last night, he said he was sending an ILOG that would explain. But we never got it."

"Did he say what was in it?"

"No. Not really."

Detective Cali, watching Monica carefully, becomes aware of how difficult this is for her. "I think we can go into detail on this later. Will I be able to reach both of you?"

The manager offers a plan. "If I may? We've provided a room for Mrs. Hardin. We'd be happy to do the same for you, Mrs. Bradbury."

"Thank you," says Sharon. "That's nice of you."

Sharon turns her attention to Monica. She sits in a chair next to Monica and puts an arm around her. Detective Cali and the manager move toward the door conversing quietly.

A few minutes later, the manager and the detective leave the office. Sharon and Monica follow. Detective Cali shakes hands with the manager and leaves. The manager goes to the mail slots and gets a key. He waits for the right moment before he speaks to Sharon. "Here is your key, Mrs. Bradbury. You're right next to Mrs. Hardin. Our dining room is around the corner there. Please be our guests. May I get you a table?"

Sharon and Monica look at one another. Monica is the first to respond. "I'm certainly not going to be able to sleep."

Sharon speaks to the manager. "Thank you. Could we have a small, out-of-the-way table?"

"Of course. Give me a minute." He disappears in the direction of the dining room.

Sharon turns her attention to Monica. "Maybe I should put my things in the room."

"I could use a few minutes," agrees Monica.

"Go ahead." Sharon turns and looks at the man standing at the front desk. "I guess I need to register?"

"Meet you in your room," says Monica and then leaves.

Sharon picks up her bag and carries it to the front desk. The clerk waits until Monica is out of sight before he speaks to Sharon. "Mrs. Bradbury, I have something for you." After he gives her a registration card, he moves away. When he returns, he carries a small manila envelope. On the front is written, *"For Sharon Bradbury or Patrick O'Connor Only."* The clerk is very nervous. He looks around often before he speaks. "Mr. Hardin gave me this envelope and told me that I should give it to you or Mr. O'Connor only in the event of … a disaster. I was to burn it when I got a call from him in California. I hope I've done the right thing."

"I'm sure you have. Did he say anything else?"

"No. Just that … it seemed very important, so I …"

Sharon studies the envelope for several seconds, then stuffs it in her purse. She hands a bill to the clerk.

"Oh, no. Mr. Hardin was very generous."

The manager reappears from around the corner, and the clerk quickly disappears. "Your table is ready when you are, Mrs. Bradbury."

"Thanks. We'll be down in a few minutes. I just want to put my bag in the room."

Sharon rushes into her room and throws her bag on a chair. She turns on the light, closes the door, rips open the envelope, and spreads the contents out on the bed. The contents consist of six pages written in longhand, a list of names and addresses, and a map. She quickly skims the pages to see what's there and then returns to the first page.

SHARE / PAT – I really hope you'll never see this. If you do, watch your ass! It started innocently enough. I followed the HDEM leads. Apparently Dallas is the headquarters—or the brain center of whatever it is that's going on. Maybe I'm just paranoid, but I don't trust anyone. In this envelope you'll find two lists: one has the names and addresses of people I've talked to who either work for DE now or worked for them in the past. The other list is the biggie. You'll recognize several names. Some of them live right in—

Sharon is interrupted by a knock on the door. She quickly gathers up the pages, folds them, puts them back in the envelope, and jams them into her purse.

"Monica?"

From outside, "Yes."

"Come in. I'll just be a second."

Two hours later the women are on the way back to their rooms. Sharon has her arm around Monica, and they talk softly as they walk. When they arrive at Monica's door they hug before Monica goes into her room. Sharon quickly opens her own door, and turns on the light. She takes the envelope from her purse and sits on the bed before she opens it. As she does so, she notices a light flashing next to the small screen on the wall. She touches the button, and on the screen appears the message: *"Return Call to Patrick O'Connor–Access 40231."* She touches those buttons, and in a few seconds, Patrick's face appears.

"You're a tough kid to track down."

"I'm sorry. I turned off my phone. I've been with Monica. I intended to call right away, but there have been … complications. The police were here. Dennis' room was ransacked, and the cause of his death is … in their words, 'suspicious.' "

"What?"

"He left us a message. I haven't had a chance to read it all yet, but it has to do with information—or people—related to the case. He knew something might happen to him."

"Are you all right?"

"No! I'm not all right! I'm … angry and miserable! Dennis is dead! Eric's in prison! And all because of this goddamned DE. I hate it!"

"What does his message say? Do you still have it?"

"It's right here in front of me."

"Read it."

"It's too long. And there are a bunch of names and addresses that don't make any sense to me."

"Well, what's it all about? Who are they?"

"I don't know." Sharon grows impatient to be free to examine the material in detail. "I need time to read it."

"Listen, my flight arrives at 12:15 tomorrow. In the meantime, call the police. Do it now!"

"I'm okay." She turns away and speaks quietly to herself. "But they're going to get theirs."

"Sharon! Do what I say."

"Not yet."

"Sharon!"

"I'm going to the airport with Monica tomorrow morning. She's going back to be with the kids. Dennis' body will be flown home later." Sharon pauses. "12:15, you say? I'll meet you."

"Flight 803, American. Now, call the police!"

Sharon, having turned her full attention to Dennis' note, responds mechanically. "Okay. See you tomorrow." She touches a button, and the picture disappears.

XXV

IT IS EARLY MORNING IN the departure center at the Dallas Airport. Sharon watches Monica enter the passenger loading area. Monica looks back and waves before she disappears. Sharon looks at her watch—6:45. She reaches in a small bag and pulls out the envelope. She opens it, looks at the list she has prepared, replaces it, and strides toward the exit.

Outside, standing on the sidewalk in front of the terminal, Stanley waits beside his cab. Sharon sees him and quickly joins him.

Inside the cab, Sharon sits next to Stanley in the front seat. Once again she consults her list. "First stop: 8234 Manchester." Stanley pushes several keys on his dash. On a small screen appears a section of the city map with the name of the street highlighted.

Stanley frowns. "Not a very nice area."

"Can't help that. That's where we're going."

As the taxi pulls away from the curb, Sharon smiles and looks at Stanley. "What say, Mate, ready for another adventure?"

"You sure can make things interesting. But I didn't understand what you meant in your message—something about your mate being hurt?"

"He's dead. Murdered."

"Murdered?"

"That's not exactly what the police say, but that's what happened. And I'm here to prove it."

"How you gonna' do that?"

"Good question."

The cab slows and comes to a stop in front of a tired and worn out four-story building with an equally drab sign in front that reads, *The Camellia Hotel.* Sharon and Stanley both get out and look around.

"Not what you'd call a high price neighborhood, Stanley."

"No. I'm coming with you."

"Thanks, but I have to do this on my own."

"Not a good idea," says Stanley.

"Maybe not, but that's the way it's going to be."

Reluctantly, Stanley sits back on his fender and folds his arms as he watches Sharon walk to the front door and enter. Inside the entry hall, she carefully looks at the boxes before pushing the button below one. After a few seconds, an angry voice sounds, "Yeah?"

"Mr. Anderson?"

"Yeah."

"My name is Sharon Bradbury. I'm a friend of Dennis Hardin. The two of you had some business recently. May I come up?"

"I don't know you."

"No, but Mr. Hardin said you'd see me." This is followed by a long silence. Sharon speaks again. "Mr. Anderson?"

"I never should have talked to him in the first place."

"I only have a couple of questions."

"It'll cost you."

"Okay."

A full minute elapses before the safety latch opens. Sharon enters and mounts the stairs. Inside a dingy hallway on the second floor, she stops in front of a graffittied door with the number ten dangling from a nail. She knocks and the door immediately opens a crack, the distance allowed by the safety latch, revealing a piece of the man on the other side.

"Mr. Anderson?"

"You alone?"

"Yes."

"What do you want?"

"Just to talk to you for a minute."

He eyes her suspiciously and closes the door. In a flash, the door swings open and he pulls Sharon inside. He quickly looks up and down the hall, then closes and bolts the door before he turns to face Sharon. The room is dirty and smelly. The only furniture consists of an unmade bed and one chair. A pile of clothes rests on a box in the corner. Anderson is wearing only boxer shorts, and though he is short and rather frail, he is remarkably menacing. His raspy smoker's voice growls, "Make it quick!"

"I ... uh ... I need the information you gave Mr. Hardin."

"Why not get it from him?"

"He left town. But he said I could talk to you."

"I don't talk to nobody for nothin'."

Sharon reaches in her pocket and produces some folded bills. She peels off a few and hands them to him. He grabs them, counts them, and puts them in the pocket of a pair of pants in the clothes pile. He quickly adds, "I told him all I know."

"He told me I wouldn't believe it unless I heard it from you. How do you know about DE?"

Anderson lights a cigarette, moves to the window, and peers out the blinds. "I useta' work for them."

"Them? Who?"

"The Society."

"That's what Dennis said, but just who and what is that?"

Anderson turns and stares at Sharon. His eyes re-evaluate. "What the hell is this all about?"

"The 'Society' controls the manufacture and sale of the HiDEMs. Right?"

"Shit yes."

"And they create the need for them?"

"Smart girl."

"Giving them a total monopoly on all sales."

"What the fuck you talkin' about?"

"That's the plan isn't it?"

Anderson studies Sharon before he speaks. "I'll be goddamned! You got no fuckin' idea!"

"No, I guess I don't."

"Shit! Whata' you, a teacher?"

"A parent."

"Okay, well then let's leave it at that, lady. They're making too goddamn much money."

Sharon, shocked at her own confusion, backs up and leans on the door. "There's more, isn't there? Tell me! What are they doing to my son?"

"Lady, you shouldnta' come here. You already got more'n your money's worth. Get outta' here. Now!" He unbolts the door.

Desperate, Sharon puts her hand on the door to keep it closed. "Wait! This 'Society.' How do I—"

"That's it! Out!"

Anderson takes her by her arm and shoves her out. Sharon turns and sticks her foot in the door jam. She looks directly at him with total resolve. "They can make those kids do anything they want … can't they!"

"You'll see in November."

"What?"

Anderson, now insanely nervous, forms a fist and threatens Sharon with it. "Leave me alone, lady! And for Christ's sake, you never heard of me!"

Stanley meets Sharon at the front door of the hotel. She remains stunned and appears numb to what is going on around her. Though concerned, he is reluctant to talk to her because of the grim look on her face. Only after she is safely seated in the cab does he probe for information. "What happened? Are you all right?"

As if locked in a trance, she simply refers to her list, remaining focused on it for several seconds. When she finally speaks, it is with a normal voice.

"Who is Howard Garman?"

Confused, Stanley says, "What?"

"Howard Garman. Do you know that name?"

"Senator Garman? Sure. He lives here in Dallas."

"What about Ted Marmoody?"

"Ted Marmoody? He's the Secretary of Education, I think. Why?"

"My God. Andrew Wycoff?"

"Just the richest man in Texas. Lives here in Dallas, too. Wanna' see his mansion? It's a bit of a trip."

"Maybe later. I've got a few more places to go first."

"Okay. Where to?"

With a blazing sun directly overhead, the cab pulls up to the curb in front of the airline terminal. Stanley starts to get out, but Sharon puts her hand on his shoulder.

"Are you busy this afternoon?"

"Not really."

"Want to keep this beautiful relationship going?"

"You bet."

"Get some lunch. I'm meeting my mate from Monterey." She looks at her watch. "I'll meet you back here at 1:20 sharp. Okay?"

Sharon leans against a wall, watching the arriving passengers emerge from a tunnel. When she sees Patrick, she smiles and waits for him to see her. When he does, he heads in her direction. After they hug, Patrick begins his rapid-fire questions. "Are you okay? How's Monica? What have you been up to?"

Sharon simply smiles, takes his arm, and directs him toward an airport restaurant close by.

Later, they sit at a small table. Sharon works on a hot dog, and Patrick has his cup of coffee. He is absorbed in a study of Dennis' notes as Sharon watches him. He looks up and sighs deeply before speaking. "This is really something. You know, we're both going to look more than a little crazy."

"Why? With all this?"

"It adds up to a lot of nothing."

"Nothing!"

"What do we have? A phrase, 'Order is important. Follow the leader,' or however it goes. So they use brainwashing. So what? How else can they create attitudes? We may not like DE, but the American people sure support the results. It may not be completely healthy as you and I define it, but it's not illegal. So somebody makes a profit. Most people call that American ingenuity."

"But this information—"

"Vague accusations from some disgruntled former employees. What exactly did they say? What evidence do we have? Even Dennis admitted it was only speculation. It doesn't add up to anything we can use."

"And what about Dennis? You don't think he was murdered? I *know* someone tried to kill me. There's more here than just greed."

"Okay, you're probably right, but what is it? How are we going to tie all this together?"

"I don't know. But I'm certainly not going to quit."

"Of course not ... but where we go from here is ... tough. I've always counted on the courts in the past."

"They're not doing us much good now."

"You're probably right. And that's really hard for me to say."

"I know."

Unnoticed by both Sharon and Patrick, two men, both about thirty and dressed in business suits, have approached and stand next to their table. The taller of the two speaks first. "Sharon Bradbury?"

Wide-eyed, Sharon looks up, fearing another crisis. "Yes."

"I'm Detective Stevens. Detective Cali asked us to escort you to the station."

"Why?"

"Some new information has come to our attention, and we'd like your input."

"Now?" asks Sharon.

"Please. May I assume this is Mr. O'Connor?"

"I'm Patrick O'Connor." He reaches out and shakes hands with the detective.

The man introduces his companion. "This is Detective Arzino. We'd appreciate it if you would also accompany us, Mr. O'Connor."

"Certainly, but I wonder if you'd be a little more specific as to why Mrs. Bradbury is requested to go to the station."

The detective explains. "We weren't given any of the details other than it has something to do with Mr. Hardin's death."

Patrick remains seated but continues, "Did I hear correctly? You're both detectives?"

"That's right."

"With the Dallas Police Department?"

"Yes, sir."

"Then I'm sure you won't mind showing me your badges."

The two men look at one another before they drop the pretense. The man identified as Detective Stevens opens his coat to reveal a revolver. "All right, if you want to make this difficult."

Sharon, now aware of what's going on, joins the fray. "What the hell is this all about? Who are you?"

"Lady, keep your voice down and do what we say."

Sharon, her ire fully aroused, speaks even louder. "Or what!"

The other man, identified as Detective Arzino, pulls close to Sharon. "Shut up. We can take care of this right here and now. And don't think for one minute we won't."

Patrick intercedes. "What is it you gentlemen want, exactly?"

"Someone wants to talk to you, that's all."

"Then why couldn't he do it right here?" inquires Patrick.

The first detective takes Patrick by the arm and lifts him from his seat. "We're through foolin' around. Either come with us quietly, or we'll drag you out of here!"

The four leave the terminal and walk toward a car parked in a yellow zone where another man, sitting in the driver's seat, awaits their arrival. When they reach a point within sight of Stanley's cab, Sharon drops her purse and sneaks a peek in his direction as she bends to pick it up. After she straightens up, she turns to the taller detective, folds her arms in front of her, and refuses to continue. He grabs her arm and pulls her in the direction of the waiting car. When they arrive, Patrick and Sharon are shoved into the back seat. The taller man sits in the front seat while the other man sits with Sharon and Patrick in the back.

Unseen by anyone in the group, Stanley, sitting in his cab, sees all of this. Confused, he does not react immediately. Finally, with his eye on the car as it eases into traffic, he pulls away from the curb, intent on following them.

The group in the first car moves along in silence. When it stops at a light, the driver, a man with a mustache, speaks. "The information Hardin gave you—do you have it with you?"

Sharon immediately answers, feigning innocence. "I don't know what you're talking about."

With the car on automatic drive, the man with a mustache turns to face Sharon. "We know better."

"And just who are you?" asks Sharon.

"The police."

Patrick jumps in. "We've already been through all that. We know you're not the police. Now who are you?" The driver does not answer. He merely focuses on the street ahead.

Sharon, with an equal mix of anger and fear, shouts, "Stop this car now!"

"I knew you were going to be a pain in the ass from the start," says the driver.

Patrick attempts to reduce the tension and appeal to reason. "Gentlemen, there must be some mistake here. Stop the car and—"

"Shut up!" the driver interrupts. "Give me your purse, lady."

The man in the back seat grabs Sharon's purse and hands it to the tall man in front. From it he pulls out Dennis' envelope. He takes a quick look at the contents. "Is this everything?" As the car slows for a crosswalk, Sharon, from her position in the middle of the back seat, reaches across Patrick, opens the door, and pushes him out. The man in front quickly jumps out and grabs Patrick before he can get to his feet. He shoves him back inside as the man in back gets a firm hold on Sharon's arm.

From his cab, Stanley watches all of this with alarm. Helpless, he bangs his fist on the steering wheel and looks around for anything or anyone he might use to intervene. Nothing.

In the other car, Patrick continues an appeal to reason. "Just stop the car, let us out, and we'll not say a thing."

"Shut up!"

Patrick asks, "Where are you taking us?" No response from any of the three men.

Losing patience, and now openly defiant, Sharon tries another approach. "You won't get an answer from these cretins. They're nobody."

"Shut up!"

"Is that all you can say, you simple shit? It's obvious you're nothing but a flunky who can't do a damned thing but carry out orders. No use talking to these idiots, Patrick."

Patrick places his hand on Sharon's arm and quietly advises, "Sharon, quiet."

Sharon continues, "Be quiet? Are you worried that we're going to hurt their feelings?"

The man with mustache turns and looks at Sharon. "Lady, I'm not gonna' warn you again."

"Or you'll do what? Put us in some stupid box? Take away our freedoms? Hell, your whole damned DE scheme is about to fall flat on its ass. I know all about your November plan, and so do a bunch of other people. You're finished!"

Patrick squeezes her arm tightly in a futile attempt to quiet her.

The man with the mustache turns to Sharon. "I'd say you're the one who's finished."

Stanley, all the while looking around, spots a patrol car coming toward them in the opposite lane. Instantly he accelerates his car and 'aims' it at the rear of the group's car ahead. An enormous crunch follows as the taxi slams into the rear end, ramming their car into a parked vehicle.

The police car makes a quick u-turn, slows, and pulls to the curb. Two officers emerge and approach the car, as does Stanley.

Two air bags in front and a huge air bag in back 'pin' the occupants to their seats. When the officers arrive, they open the doors, and the people inside slowly get out. The man with the mustache gets out of the driver's seat. He screams at Stanley. "You son-of-a-bitch!"

Stanley smiles and shrugs his shoulders. "Sorry. The probacon stuck. Nothing I could do."

The driver points to a crushed rear end and a flat tire. "Goddammit! Look at that!"

Finally able to crawl out from under the bag in back, Sharon sees Stanley for the first time and gives him a big smile. She immediately retrieves her purse from the front seat, grabs Patrick's hand, and pulls him toward the cab. With the officers present, the men in the car are powerless to stop them. Sharon and Patrick climb inside the cab and close the doors.

The first officer speaks to the drivers of the two vehicles. "All right, gentlemen, IDEX numbers please." From his wallet, Stanley produces a card. The other driver, all the while glaring at Sharon and Patrick as they enter the cab, does the same.

The officer hands the cards to his partner and asks him to run a check on them. His partner slides the cards through a slot in a device on the dashboard of the police car, manipulates the controls, and waits for a printout. In a matter of seconds the results appear. He looks at the other officer and announces, "MMR-882 and PFR-441."

Stanley's apology, dripping with sarcasm, is offered. "I'm really sorry, mister. It wasn't my fault."

"Yeah, yeah!"

From inside the police car, the officer provides the required code. "Okay, checks out. CR-816." The first officer concludes their business. "That's it, gentlemen. You heard? Your file number is CR-816. You'll receive a report and a notification as to the time and place you're to appear. Any questions?"

Stanley is most polite. "No, sir. Thank you." He starts to leave. The other driver voices his objection. "Wait a minute! He can't leave! Look at my tire!"

"We'll get you a tow. There's no reason for him to stay. Everything's been recorded."

Helpless, the man with the mustache stands watching Stanley hop in the car and ease it away from the curb. As they pass, Stanley waves demurely.

Thirty minutes later, a safe distance away, the cab is parked under the shade of a tree in a quiet park. The three, seeking relief from the heat, sit on the grass under the shade of another tree.

Stanley looks at the damage to the front end of his vehicle. "I'd appreciate knowing what the hell I just did."

"You saved our ass," says Sharon.

"From what? What's going on?"

"That's gonna take a while," offers Sharon. "We owe you a chunk of money for repairs."

"That would be nice," says Stanley. "Do you remember what you said when we first met? 'You trust me, and I'll trust you,' "

Patrick adds his voice. "I assume this is the Aussie mate you told me about. Sure nice to meet you. The truth is, Stanley, if you hadn't been there, the two of us would probably have ended up dead. We certainly owe you an explanation, but our most immediate problem is figuring out where we go from here. Getting home for us is not going to be easy."

"That's right," adds Sharon. "We can't—"

Patrick finishes her thought. "We can't use an airline—or the rails—or a bus. They'll be all over everything. And we're due in court in two days."

Sharon flashes a triumphant smile. "Is this enough evidence for you? Still think I'm off my trolly?"

"Not after this," admits Patrick.

"Who were those guys?" asks Stanley.

"They certainly *weren't* the police," says Patrick.

Sharon continues Patrick's thought, expressing her confusion. "No, they weren't, so who can we trust?"

"That's why I'm not sure about going to them now—the police that is. I don't know how deep this goes. We've got to figure out a way to do this on our own."

He looks at Stanley. "How long you been a cabbie, Stanley?"

"Three years, give or take."

"Got a lot of stories, I'll bet."

"This one's gonna be right up there."

Patrick, his plan now formulated, continues to question Stanley. "Ever been to California?"

"Once, when I was a kid."

"Like to do it again?"

"I get it. Might be our best bet," says Sharon.

Stanley begins to understand. "Are you talking about ..."

"You *are* a taxi driver, aren't you, Mate?"

"Well, yeah," replies Stanley. "You wanna drive all the way?"

Patrick asks, "How long would it take?"

"Geez, I dunno. Maybe ... fifteen—twenty hours. Are you serious? In my cab?"

Sharon continues to quiz Stanley. "You could do it couldn't you?"

"Well, I could do it, but ... don't you think they'd know about this cab?"

"Of course," answers Patrick, "but you do have another car, don't you?"

"Sure."

"Then, how about it?"

With the car on automatic drive, Stanley dozes in the front seat. Sharon and Patrick, in the back seat, stare out the window at the black night.

Sharon is the first to speak. "Figure out what we're gonna do when we get back?"

"It's about time for the prosecution to turn the case over to us. I've been sitting here trying to figure out just how to handle it."

"That's not what I'm talking about."

Patrick turns to look at Sharon. "Just exactly what are you talking about?"

"Do you really think you have a chance in court?"

"Not much of one, no."

"Then maybe it's time for me to get Eric and get out of the mess on my own."

"And just how do you propose to do that? Walk in, politely ask for permission to have him home for Thanksgiving?"

"Might be a tad more difficult than that."

"Share ... I've been thinking about something you said."

"What?"

"In the car with those men you said something about a 'November Plan.'"

"I was just baiting them."

"So you made it up?"

"No. It was something Anderson said. I was trying to get some kind of reaction."

"Anderson mentioned a 'November Plan'?"

"I really don't remember if he actually said 'November Plan'... now that I think about it ... he said something like, 'you'll find out in November.'"

"Find out what? Was it in response to something you said?"

"I was pretty emotional at the time. I had just realized that they—DE—could make the kids do whatever they wanted them to."

"And he said, 'You'll find out in November?'"

"I think so. Doesn't make any sense, does it?"

"Of course it does. How could we have been so stupid? It was right in front of us all the time."

"What?"

"We elect a president in November."

XXVI

WITH THE CAR PARKED AT a scenic viewpoint overlooking the Pacific Ocean, Sharon, Patrick, and Stanley stand watching the first rays of the sun peek over the mountains to the east.

Sharon speaks to Stanley. "What do you think, Mate?"

"Mighty pretty."

Patrick weighs in. "God's country."

"Remind you a bit of Perth?"

"You know, it does. Can't say I spent a lot of time watching the sun come up, but it does make me a little homesick. Where do we go from here?"

"Another couple of hours and we'll be there. Then we'll settle up, and you can be on your way."

"So," says Stanley, "tell me one more time, why it is I can't help?"

"We've been through all that," explains Sharon.

Patrick adds, "It's not your fight."

"I been thinking about that." Stanley speaks slowly, but firmly. "I'm there when Sharon gets all this goin', whatever it is … I rescue both of you from the bad guys … drive you from Dallas to Monterey … and I'm not involved?"

Sharon smiles and looks at Patrick. "Told ya you can't keep these Aussie blokes from stickin' their noses in where they don't belong. It's a damn good plan. Should we?"

Patrick carefully studies Stanley, and then squints as he looks in the direction of the sunrise. "Give him his day in the sun? Sure!"

Sharon smiles at Stanley and offers an Australian bump, a fist with the thumb up. Stanley bumps it with his own as she turns and speaks to Patrick. "Maybe you can explain what's going on to him. I've gotta make a call." She leaves them and returns to the car, finds her purse, and pulls out her cell phone. After that she walks away from the car in the direction of the rising sun. She pushes a button on the phone and speaks into it. "Starfish 8847."

A few seconds later a voice answers, "Not available—leave a message."

"Helen, this is Sharon Bradbury. Please call me back as soon as you hear this. I need your help."

XXVII

IT IS MID-MORNING ON A trail near the Webber home. Paul jogs through a stand of trees. A voice interrupts his concentration. "Dad ... Dad!" He stops, looks in the direction of the voice, and sees a piece of Sharon hidden behind a tree.

"Sharon?" He starts to move in her direction.

In a loud whisper, Sharon stops him. "Stay where you are! Don't look this way. Do some stretching—anything. Someone may be watching you. I know this sounds crazy, but do as I say. I've got to stay out of sight."

Though thoroughly confused, Paul does as he is directed.

Sharon continues, "I really need your help, Dad. There's an envelope inside a newspaper at the end of the trail near the house. Read it very carefully, and please, follow the directions."

"Sharon, I—"

"Not now, Dad. It's too dangerous. Trust me." Paul finishes his stretching and continues his run.

In a tiny all-night coffee shop in Pacific Grove, Sharon sits in a booth having a cup of coffee. It is after midnight, and she is the only customer there. Paul enters, sees Sharon, and walks to her booth. He gives her a kiss and slides into a seat.

"How are you, sweetheart?"

"I'm okay. Were you—"

"Don't worry. I'm a pretty clever fellow. There's no way anyone could have followed me. I was so sneaky I almost got lost. Sorry I was a little late."

"I was afraid you'd think I was bonkers."

"Why aren't you staying at home?"

"It's too dangerous. I'm sure the house is being watched."

"Where are you staying then?"

"With Lynn."

"Do you really think we can pull this off?"

"You said 'we.' Then you're willing to help?"

"Of course. Why wouldn't I?"

"Did you get the tickets?"

"Too dangerous. If this is all true, a commercial aircraft is out of the question. I have a friend who owns a plane. He owes me a big favor. He agreed to fly you to Canada."

"Canada?"

"You can't go home. They'd have no trouble finding you there."

"Then you do …"

"Of course I believe you. It's sure a 'ripper of a yarn' though—is that how you say it?"

"Hey, you're a bit o' all right. I'll make an Aussie out of you yet. But this Canada thing. I don't know."

"I've even made arrangements there. Some friends are more than happy to help."

"Okay. I'll be guided by your judgment on Canada for a while, but we'll be going back to Australia later. Not to the ranch of course, but we've got lots of friends there. We'll be fine."

"You really think this plan of yours will work?"

"I think it's pretty damn clever."

"Why don't you want my car?"

"It's best to keep you and mom out of this as much as we can. I think there'll be some people mighty surprised to see us in court today. Until then, we're staying completely out of sight. And today we have to make everything look as normal as possible."

"You mentioned some other people in your note. Who are they?"

"There's Stanley—remember, I told you about him? The taxi driver I met in Dallas. He drove us all the way from Texas. Saved our lives back there. He's a real mate. Then there's Helen and Martin. Remember the couple I met when I was shopping with mom? They belong to a group called *Save the Children*. I called them, and they're helping a lot. They've arranged for the two cars we're using. And Patrick, of course."

"Are you sure he's up to it?"

"Are you kidding? He's totally into this. It's as much his plan as it is mine. He's got more energy than all of us put together. Did you know he got hit with a contempt of court penalty—or citation—or whatever it's called? Funny thing is, he loved it! Said it made him feel like a kid again."

"Nothing funny about that," says Paul. "That's serious."

"Not to Patrick. It was like a badge of honor to him. Said he'd have 'taken a shot at a little jail time' if he didn't think he'd be thrown off the case."

"Anybody else?"

"Well, there's Lynn."

"She's involved too?"

"Yeah. Crazy, huh? I tried to keep her out of it, but she wouldn't take no for an answer. She hates this damned DE as much as I do."

"You sure the DE people will let it go?"

"They'll probably be happy as hell to get rid of us."

"I hope so."

"I'd better get going." Sharon eases out of the booth. "Patrick and I have to be in court in a few hours. He's at Lynn's now working on his presentation. But it's all arranged for tonight—at least from our end. Is that okay for you?"

"That's the way I set it up."

An hour later, Sharon enters Lynn's beach cottage. Stanley is asleep on the couch in the living room, and Patrick is studying a brief at a desk next to the window. He looks up, puts down his pen, and speaks in a loud whisper.

"How'd it go?"

"Fine. Dad even arranged for a private plane that belongs to a friend of his. But, it's taking us to Canada."

"Canada? Just as well. Is everything else set? The cars?"

"Helen and Martin are taking care of that. They'll be waiting for us just outside the school. I've checked with her several times. They've been great."

"Well … okay." Patrick looks puzzled. "Just seems strange they'd be willing to do so much."

"They know how awful DE is," explains Sharon. "Said how sorry they were about Dennis."

"What?"

"They're willing do to anything against those bastards."

"No. What did you say about Dennis?"

"Said she was really sorry about our loss."

"Did you tell her about Dennis?"

Several seconds elapse before Sharon answers. "No. I didn't."

XXVIII

IT IS A LITTLE PAST midnight. Sharon, dressed in an attendant's white uniform, pushes a cart down the hall on the third floor of the school. She arrives at Room 306, eases the door open, and looks around. The technician's back is toward her, so she watches for several seconds before backing out.

On the fourth level, Stanley enters a room marked *Utility*. A single attendant, at the other end of the room, is at work folding laundry. Stanley looks at a sheet posted on the wall and then at his watch. He moves farther into room, looking around as he goes. Finally, he speaks. "Mary? Mary Ellis?"

The attendant looks around and finds Stanley with her eyes. "Yes?"

"Hi. You're supposed to report to your supervisor's office."

"Me? Now? What for?"

"Just delivering a message. They told me to take your place until you come back."

The worried attendant appeals to Stanley, "I didn't do anything!"

"Probably just an evaluation."

"I had one a couple of weeks ago. Why now?"

"Hey, I'm just delivering a message."

The attendant drops the towel she was folding and moves toward the door, shaking her head. Stanley watches her disappear and then checks his watch again. Immediately after she exits, Patrick enters.

Mary Ellis knocks on the door marked *Personnel*. From inside, a voice sounds, "Come in." She does as instructed. The man, seated behind a desk, frowns and seeks the reason for her presence. "What is it?"

"I was told to report to you."

"Who are you?"

"Mary Ellis, sir."

"What's this about? Who told you to report?"

"Another attendant. A man. I don't know his name."
"And he didn't say why?"
"No."
"Where do you work?"
"Section four."
"Take a seat. Let me finish this, and then we'll go see what this is all about."

From underneath a pile of towels in a laundry cart, Stanley pulls out a five-gallon can. He removes the cap and pours a substance on the pile of towels in the cart. Patrick lights a match and drops it on the pile. It quickly ignites.

Throughout the school a loud, steady alarm bell sounds. Instantly, the cubicles rotate 180 degrees. As they come to a stop, their fronts slowly rise. The children step outside and stand motionless by their pods. In room 306 Sharon waits and watches Eric's cubicle. As soon as he steps outside, she moves toward him. She does so with tears running down her cheeks as she looks into the lifeless faces of the children. When she reaches Eric, she puts her hands on his shoulders and directs him toward the door. Just as they arrive, it opens.

The personnel officer, with Mary Ellis at his side, confronts Sharon. He is the first to speak. "What are you doing? Who are you?"

"Don't worry, I'm leaving right now."

"Take that child back now."

"Not likely!"

As Sharon attempts to push past him, he grabs her arm and tries to restrain her. At that moment, Patrick and Stanley appear, pushing a cart. The instant Stanley sees the struggle taking place, he picks up a fire extinguisher from the cart and clubs Sharon's assailant from behind. The man crumples to the floor. Stanley picks up Eric and gently places him in the middle of the pile of towels and covers him. Patrick peeks outside the room, and then beckons the others to follow.

Helplessly, Sharon stands looking at the children. Stanley grabs her hand and pulls her toward the door. Once outside, they quickly move down the hall, past several other attendants looking around for the problem, and enter an elevator. When it opens on the first floor, they move toward the door marked *Emergency Exit*. Before they are able to go more than a few feet, two security guards appear running down the hall from the opposite direction. The group watches them arrive and take a position in front of the exit.

Stanley is the first to react. He does an immediate about-face with the cart and heads out of the guards' sight. His two companions quickly follow. In their frantic search for an avenue of escape they again pass a number of confused attendants. Suddenly, a familiar voice halts Sharon in her tracks. "Mrs. Bradbury!" She looks around for its source and sees an attendant heading towards them.

It takes a second for Sharon's senses to process the image. "Robert! What are you doing here?"

Robert offers a weak smile. "It's where I work, remember?"

During the brief and somewhat awkward silence that follows, Robert sees Sharon's two companions with the towel cart and does a little processing of his own. He motions for Sharon to follow and then hurries down the corridor. Sharon, with the other two close behind, does as instructed.

Robert turns a corner and moves down a short hallway toward an unmarked door. After he arrives he swipes a card through the slot and the door opens. The understanding that follows when Robert and Sharon's eyes meet requires no words other than Robert's warning. "You'd better hurry!"

A giant smile light Sharon's face before she reaches out to hug Robert and give him a big kiss.

Parked on a side street around the corner from the school, two cars await the escapees. A woman, dressed in a white warm-up suit, with her hand on a young boy's shoulder, approach the cars.

When they arrive, the doors open and Thornberg, Helen, and three men step out to confront the pair.

Thornberg's booming voice breaks the silence. "Good evening, Sharon. I see your son is with you."

The woman stops and pulls back the hood of her warm-up. "Are you speaking to me? My name is Lynn. This is my *ten-year old* nephew. Who are you?"

Shocked, Thornberg turns to one of the men and shouts, "Turn on the lights!" The man climbs into the car next to him and does as he was directed, illuminating the pair.

Lynn puts her arm around her nephew, reaches in her pocket, and pulls out a cell phone. She quickly punches a few buttons and shouts, "Police! Help, we're being attacked!"

With Stanley behind the wheel, the car speeds toward the Monterey Airport. In the back seat next to Patrick, Sharon tenderly holds Eric in her arms. There is no response. He merely stares straight ahead.

Kristen, Paul, and a squirmy Brock stand next to a private hangar at the airport watching the road. A pair of headlights rounds the corner, and the three anxiously step out to look. The car pulls next to the chain link fence and stops at the gate. Stanley is the first to exit. He and Sharon then help Eric out of the car and head toward the gate. Patrick is close behind.

Kristen almost screams in delight. "Sharon, you got Eric!"

Brock, accompanied by a very old friend, runs to the gate, and the grandparents hurry behind him. When he reaches the fugitives, Brock shouts, "Hey, Eric!" and raises his hand for a high five. When Eric fails to respond, Brock lifts Eric's hand and smacks his own against it. Standing at Brock's side, with his tail wagging at full speed and anxious to be in the center of the activity, is Buns. He licks Eric's hand and searches with his nose for familiar scents.

Very slowly, Eric drops to his knees, allowing Buns to cover his face with a loving tongue. A broad smile and a look of recognition replaces the blank exterior that had been Eric's face.

"Hey, Buns." Then he looks directly at Brock and asks, "How's it goin', Brock? Finally he notices Sharon's beaming face. "Hi, Mom."

A few minutes later everyone is gathered next to the small jet. Sharon puts her arms around Patrick and gives him a kiss. "Patrick O'Connor, you're really something! I'll never forget the way you looked flying down the hall pushing that cart. I didn't know you could move that fast."

"Neither did I."

She takes a step back and looks directly into his eyes as she searches for the right words. "Patrick, I …"

"I know. Me, too."

Stanley, somewhat apart from the rest, quietly watches and waits. When Sharon turns to him, he offers a weak smile. Sharon takes his arm. "Remember what you said about going home one of these days? How about now?"

"What?" asks Stanley.

"You might have to put up with Canada for a while, but hell, I figure you can handle anything."

"You mean, go with you now?"

"Why not? What else you got goin'?"

A big grin provides his answer. As he hurries toward his car, he yells, "Gotta get my bag."

Paul returns from his meeting with the pilot. "You better get going, honey. We don't want to push our luck too far."

" I should be here with you two to fight this thing out," says Sharon.

"You and your mother will have your hands full with those two grandsons of mine."

"Why can't you come with us?"

Patrick weighs in. "It's got to be done from here. We'll just finish the job you started."

"But how?" asks Sharon. "What can you do?"

"Get the information to the right people," explains Patrick.

"Who's that?"

Patrick smiles. "An old fart like me has managed a few relationships with some pretty influential people."

"And don't forget," adds Paul, "your dad still knows some heavy hitters—and I'm not talking about golf."

"But it's too dangerous!"

"I've taken care of that. They'll never find us where we're going."

Sharon, refusing to give up, starts to say, "I' can—"

Patrick stops her with, "If we need you to testify, we'll let you know. But only if it's safe. Just be sure you keep your copy of the report in a secure place."

"But—"

"Enough of this," says Paul. "You belong with those kids. Now get going."

Sharon finally gives in to the wisdom of their argument. She puts her arm around her dad and gives him a kiss. He returns her affection by caressing her cheek lovingly.

As the two men watch the plane begin its taxi run, they finalize their plans. "Where's your car?" asks Patrick.

"We parked it out of sight a couple of blocks away. I'll go get it. Can you drive Lynn's car?"

"Sure. I'll get the stuff they left and put it in her car while you're gone. Hurry back."

"Okay." Paul turns and jogs toward his car.

Minutes later, just as Paul arrives at the car, the approaching sound of two cars traveling very fast captures his attention. He ducks down behind his as they race by him. He quickly gets in, starts the car and, with the lights off, slowly moves toward the gate.

Patrick stands next to Lynn's car watching the plane take off. The instant he hears the cars screech to a halt, he runs through the opening in the gate and heads in the direction of a group of workers in the distance.

Paul's car continues to approach the gate. It comes to an immediate stop when two gunshots break the silence of the night. Paul opens his door, steps out, and is able to see two men inside the enclosure carrying a body toward the gate. Helplessly, Paul can only watch in horror as he sees the two carry Patrick's lifeless body to the car and toss it in the back seat before they speed away.

Five hours later the sun is just making its appearance. Bartleby, unshaven and casually dressed, is seated in Thornberg's office. Thornberg stands at the window staring out at the ocean.

"So," questions Bartleby, "They just walked in, got the kid, and walked out?"

"It appears so, yes."

"But—"

"But what? This isn't a prison. Parents are permitted to come and go as they please," explains Thornberg. .

"The parents, but not the kids! Can we catch them?"

"Maybe. I doubt it."

With a touch of dread in his voice, Bartleby asks, "You call Dallas?"

"First thing."

"What'd they say?"

"They sure as hell weren't happy. They're afraid she can cause all kinds of trouble." After some thought, Thornberg adds, "But what does she really know?"

"If she knows anything, that's too much for Dallas."

"That's true."

Bartleby continues, "You think they're on their way to Australia?"

"Of course," replies Thornberg, "But that'll be difficult for them. We're tapped into all the airlines and ships. At least we got rid of the old crank professor. She'll have to be careful, or we'll get her."

A little more than a week later, in a conference room in the Russell Senate Office building in Washington D.C., Paul is seated at a table on which rests three folders.

The door opens, and three well-dressed men enter. Paul stands and walks around the table to greet them. "Thank you for your time, Senators. I'm Paul Webber, Mrs. Bradbury's father. This is the report compiled by Mr. O'Connor I spoke to you about."

IN THE SPACIOUS KITCHEN OF a cabin in New South Wales, Sharon, Eric, Brock, and Kristen are seated at the kitchen table having dinner. Paul has already finished and sits reading his *Newsview* in a chair next to the window in the living room, adjacent to the kitchen. A small television sitting on the kitchen counter plays quietly in the background, but they pay little attention to it. "Would tomorrow be all right?" asks Eric.

"Sure," says Sharon. "I'll pick you two up after your game." She gets up and goes to the sink to begin the dishes.

Kristen adds, "He could stay all weekend if he likes. That would be okay, wouldn't it?"

"Of course," answers Sharon.

Pleased and excited by the adults' approval, Eric expresses his gratitude. "Thanks."

Brock, eager to join in the fun, asks, "Can we go riding?"

"I don't know why not?" says Kristen. "You two are certainly good with horses."

"You wanna come, Grammy?" asks Eric.

Kristen laughs and offers an excuse. "Oh, I think I'll pass on that. I need to help your mom, and I don't want to slow you boys down."

Brock, eager to be taken seriously as a horseman, assures his grandmother, "You'd love it. You said you'd let us teach you how."

"And I will ... someday."

As the conversation continues, Sharon becomes interested in the news on the television when she hears a reference made to world news. She focuses on the story being reported.

"... from around the world. In the United States the scandal surrounding the DE program continues to accelerate. The list of prominent names implicated in this shocking expose' grows by the hour. Senators Howard Garman and Harold Andrews continue to refuse to comment on the charges leveled at them by the Senate's investigating committee."

148

A film clip of the two men exiting a car, with a host of reporters waiting, appears on the screen.

Paul lowers his *Newsview,* listens briefly before he rises and moves to a position where he can see the screen. Sharon becomes aware of his presence, and their eyes meet briefly as the report continues.

"—Nobel prize winner Sheldon Keppard—"

Now on the screen is a clip of Dr. Keppard receiving his award at the ceremony in Stockholm.

"—and the United States Secretary of Education, Ted Marmoody, continue to insist that the charges are false."

Marmoody's face fills the screen as he stands before a bank of microphones.

"These charges are ridiculous. I welcome the opportunity to clear my name."

"All have been indicted on charges of criminal fraud as a result of their alleged tampering with the revolutionary system of education popularly referred to as DE. The extent of their alleged criminal involvement is still under investigation."

Again, Sharon and Paul exchange a look. Sharon smiles broadly and raises her fist, signaling victory. "Yes!"

"In spite of these charges, the image of DE appears to remain unscathed. An enormous groundswell of support has erupted across the country."

Scenes of marchers carrying placards are shown. All the signs indicate enthusiastic support for the program. A man from the crowd is stopped and asked to comment. "This attack on DE is criminal! It's saved this great nation of ours!"

Another view is presented, this time from a woman, "I don't know anything about what these people are accused of doing, but I certainly remember what it was like before DE, and I'll do anything I can to protect it."

Back to the newsperson in the television studio as the report is concluded. "The revolutionary educational program remains an integral part of the hearts and minds of Americans all across the country. Dr. William Thornberg, one of the original developers of DE, has been named the Interim Secretary of Education until this matter is resolved. Coincidentally, in spite of indications that their Supreme Court will re-evaluate the constitutionality issue of DE, Australian officials have just returned from a visit with education experts in the United States, and plans are currently underway to experiment with this program here in Australia."

Sharon's head slowly lowers as her eyes fill with tears of frustration and anger.

A new story takes center stage: "Meanwhile, with only one week left before their presidential election, Helena Conniff maintains a slight lead over her two opponents in the polls." A brief film clip of Helena Conniff surrounded by a particularly youthful-looking crowd appears on the screen.

"In Central America, the new—"

Sharon can take it no longer. She touches the remote control, and the picture disappears. The boys, fully aware of the content of the televised message, remain discretely taciturn. Finally, Eric makes an effort to redirect her thoughts. "Mom, Brock and I challenge you to a game of 'Goofball,' okay?"

Sharon, disconcerted but trying to mask it, responds, "Okay. Let me get a few dishes done first."

Kristen, attempting to make a contribution to a change in atmosphere as well, answers the boys' challenge with a grin. "Come on, I'll give you two a lesson while your mom finishes up."

With that, she stands and walks into the living room. The boys remain seated for several seconds watching Sharon and evaluating the dynamics taking place before they rise and follow their grandmother. Paul walks to Sharon, puts his arms around her, and gives her a comforting hug. "Keep your chin up, honey. We'll get there." Sharon does her best to give him a reassuring smile in return. "I'll help your mom entertain the kids. Come in when you're done." He gently pats her behind, turns and leaves the kitchen.

Sharon remains standing at the sink mechanically completing her task as she looks out the window at the distant mountains—dark and dangerous—as they swallow the final rays of sun.

What she does not see is the car that moves slowly down the dirt road toward their house. It comes to a stop three or four hundred yards from the front gate. Three men get out and huddle together briefly before they spread out and approach the house on foot.

THE END

"Lacking the ability to impose social and cultural uniformity upon embryos, the rulers of tomorrow's over-populated and over-organized world will try to impose social and cultural uniformity upon adults and their children. To achieve this end, they will (unless prevented) make use of all the mind-manipulating techniques at their disposal and will not hesitate to reinforce these methods of non-rational persuasion by economic coercion and threats of physical violence. If this kind of tyranny is to be avoided, we must begin without delay to educate ourselves and our children for freedom and self-government."

ALDOUS HUXLEY